MW00941749

HUNGER MOON

HUNGER MOON

Sarah Lamstein

To the students at the Runkle School - Best wishes - Sarah Lamstein June 2005

FRONT STREET
Asheville, North Carolina

Printed in China
Designed by Helen Robinson

First edition

Library of Congress Cataloging-in-Publication Data

Lamstein, Sarah
Hunger Moon / by Sarah Lamstein.— 1st ed.
p. cm.
Summary: In 1953 in Chicago, Ruth struggles to deal with her parents' constant arguing, taking care of her younger brothers, one of whom is mentally disabled, and getting along in middle school.
ISBN 1-932425-05-5 (alk. paper)
[1. Family problems—Fiction. 2. Brothers and sisters—Fiction.
3. Schools—Fiction. 4. People with mental disabilities—Fiction.
5. Chicago (Ill.)—History—20th century—Fiction.] I. Title.
PZ7.L215Hu 2003
[Fic]—dc22 2003023113

For J.D.M.

ACKNOWLEDGMENTS

For being the book's first reader and for her friendship that goes nearly all the way back, I thank Judith Beth Cohen. I am most grateful for the loving counsel of those I hold closest—Joel, Josh, Emily, Abby, David, Daniel, and Ann. For their encouragement and for shining the light, I thank my advisors in the Vermont College MFA Program in Writing for Children and Young Adults—Ellen Howard, M.T. Anderson, and Jane Resh Thomas. Carolyn Coman, my editor, I thank for absolutely everything.

HUNGER MOON

Cherries hang ripe on the backyard tree. We want to get them before the robins do and make pie. When we've picked all we can, we empty our pails into a big bowl in the kitchen and then Mom and I start.

Just Mom and me make pie. I pit the cherries with a hairpin the way Mom showed me, fast, without pushing out too much juice, the way Mom likes. Mom makes the crust, blending flour, shortening, and water with a few quick squeezes. We listen to White Sox baseball on the radio. Mom likes the third baseman. Her hands move faster when he comes to bat.

Maybe I can tell Mom my news of the day about Eugene and square dancing, plus the Communists in Current Events. But we don't talk because Mom is busy working and listening to the radio. I'm working too. Mom rolls the dough with strong strokes on the wooden pastry board, then lifts it gently into the pie plate. She crimps the edges, pours in the pitted cherries, and makes a pretty lattice top. Then she pops the pie in the oven.

Like a whirlwind, Mom cleans the kitchen until it's spotless. She snaps out her apron on the back porch. Flour dust escapes into the air.

Monday night I have to feed my brothers supper because Mom and Dad work late. Verna fixes it, then catches her bus. I put it on the table.

I call out the back door, "Eddy, Isaac, Michael!" in the order of their birth. Isaac and Michael drop their sticks, Eddy puts down his chalk, and they come in the house. Not one of us washes our hands.

Monday night is stew.

Eddy chews his meat up, down, and sideways, short quick moves like a rabbit. "He's doing it," Isaac says.

Eddy has his fingers at his mouth.

Isaac's eyes blink hard behind his glasses.

Eddy takes a chewed piece of meat out of his mouth and puts it on his plate.

"Sickening!" Isaac says.

Michael looks up.

"It's hard gristle," Eddy says, his voice loud and flat. "I can't swallow it."

"Oh, be quiet," I say. "Let's just eat."

I'm tired of looking and screaming about Eddy's eating. I just want to leave it.

Eddy's still eating after the rest of us are finished.

"Bring your plate to the sink when you're done," I say. I scrub the stew pot with a Brillo until it shines. Eddy gives me his plate with two hands.

"Get on your pj's and come down for TV."

Our TV is still a miracle. We got it centuries after everyone else, last year, the Zenith model for 1953. Before, I watched at Jeanie's.

I clean the kitchen until it's spotless, the way Mom likes, and put things back where they belong. Then I get on my pj's, and we all four watch TV. Isaac and Michael want *Captain Video* at 7:00. Eddy and I like *I Love Lucy*, which comes on at 9:00.

Eddy laughs loud and hard at whatever he thinks is funny, then repeats it for the next ten minutes so none of us can hear.

"Lucy said, 'No, Ricky, I don't like bananas.' Huh, huh, huh" (that's Eddy laughing). "She said, 'I don't like bananas.' Huh, huh, huh."

"Be quiet, Eddy," I say.

"It was funny. She said, 'No, Ricky, I don't like bana—'"

Isaac socks Eddy's arm.

"Stop that!" Eddy yells. "It was funny. She said, 'Ricky ...'"

He stops right in the middle if something else catches his eye.

I want to be like Lucy. On TV. Then everyone will watch me.

In the morning, Mom combs her hair in the bathroom mirror. "I used to be beautiful," she says. She stares straight at her face.

I think Mom still is. I hope I'll be. Mom always says too bad my eyebrows are from Grandma Tepper.

After school, I go to the table in our living room that has Mark Twain books for decoration with leather covers and gold titles. I pass the piano hardly anyone plays and take *Tom Sawyer.* Miss Roberts in Library says I'd like it. Ever since kindergarten, when she read *Curious George* in her voice like a mother dove, I've believed her.

I sit in the patch of sun by the window and read. Tom's aunt tried to get him to wash. I slice some cake and take that book upstairs. Tom's friend Huck was an orphan and went around dirty. I like the part about Tom falling in love with Becky and jumping all over her fence.

I think about Eugene.

"I can't carry it," Eddy says. "My heart."

Eddy always says "my heart" when he has to run fast or lift things. He was born with a hole in his heart, which Mom says is now good and closed, and he doesn't have to say "my heart." I think Eddy was born with a hole in his head, because just about everything leaks out. Except maps. He's a genius in the map department.

I lift some papers out of Eddy's bag and pack them in mine. We're hauling in newspapers for the school paper drive, which sells them for new kickballs, stage lights for the auditorium, and things. We get our newspapers from the Stickels two doors down. Mr. and Mrs. Stickel are old and keep stacks and stacks of papers. We don't have newspapers in our house. Mom and Dad only get one Friday nights when they have time to read. They throw it out as soon as they are finished.

Eddy stops about forty times, dropping his bag and picking it up.

"We'll be tardy!" I yell. He's practically a block behind me.

Outside third grade, he drops his bag.

"Come on, Eddy," I say.

I follow him past midget desks to the back of his room, where bags of newspaper are piled. Eddy moves like a rocking boat, his stiff legs bumping him from side to side.

None of the kids say hi.

"It's heavy," Eddy says in his loud, flat voice. "My heart."

"Come on," I say.

He puts his bag on the pile, then we walk back to his locker. Slowly he unbuttons his coat, his fingers weak like a baby's.

"I'll meet you by the Boynton Avenue door at lunch," I say. Mom makes me walk him to and from school, so he won't be alone.

Eddy hangs up his coat and takes a pencil stub out of

the pocket. Mom and Dad say we have to use things to the bitter end.

I run upstairs to sixth. My locker echoes in the empty corridor. I step in just before the bell.

Miss Peterson turns her head from the board, where she's writing the day's assignments.

"Make fast footprints to your seat and pretend you're on a desert isle," she says. She goes back to the board.

Everyone looks at me. I hold my nose in the air and stick out my rear end, just like Miss Peterson. The class laughs.

I feel like Lucy on TV.

"Ruth?" Miss Peterson turns.

I hurry to the fourth row, fourth seat, with the tall kids, before Miss Peterson can say, "March back, Ruth, and let your nose say hello to the wall."

"Whose house?" Jeanie asks on the way home from school.

"Mine."

Eddy straggles behind us, his brown tie shoes scuffing the pavement. Isaac and David Stein dance ahead, like first graders do.

First we stop at Cunningham Pharmacy to buy a *True Romance* magazine. We read stories before we write them.

It helps our imaginations.

We stare at the cover of *True Romance.*

"He really loves her," I say. The man is looking at the woman with his whole face, his eyes, nose, and mouth pointed in her direction.

"We could write about that," Jeanie says. "These two people gazing at each other while things go on around them, like bank robbers, and cats and dogs falling out of trees."

Eddy pays a nickel for his chalk.

Verna has snack ready. Milk and orange cake with orange frosting. Mom bakes cakes from scratch every week, her strong arm beating the batter. Spice cake with buttercream frosting. Carrot cake with cream cheese frosting. Cherry cake with marshmallow frosting. We are a cake family, and Mom is our leader in the cake department.

Verna turns on the blender and fixes Eddy a milkshake.

"How come he gets one?" Jeanie asks me.

"Mom tells her to."

"Because he's skinny?" Jeanie asks.

Eddy doesn't seem to hear. He slurps his milkshake, his throat making loud clicks with each swallow. Then he takes his cars outside.

In my room, we write about a girl named Noreen with a big chest and a noisy family. A soldier named Norton comes each night and they kiss and embrace on the porch.

"I love you, Noreen," Norton said. He looked straight at her.

The noisy family came out.

"What?" Noreen asked.

Then they got married and drove over to a quiet meadow.

After Jeanie leaves, I sprawl out on the back porch ledge and think about Eugene. The seventh grade does square dancing with the sixth every Thursday during Gym. Maybe our arms will brush in do-si-do.

Isaac and Michael run around the back yard waving sticks. Mom and Dad say, "No toy guns for those boys." So those boys use sticks and make gun noises, *pooiy, pooiy, pshhh, psshhhh*! David Stein is over with his cap gun. They take turns using it.

Eddy inches along the concrete on his bottom, moving small cars through the city of Baltimore. He's drawn it with chalk. He knows all the streets by heart, from studying maps. He also knows the capital of every state in the United States and every country in the world. Mom says she wishes Eddy knew other things the way he knows streets and capitals.

Eddy makes green and red circles for traffic lights and yellow lines for the streets and highways. A blue wavy line is the Patapsco River. Nana's house is the only building in the city.

"*Vrrooom, vrooomm.* Red light, stop! Green light, go!" He moves his little cars through the streets.

The younger boys come over.

Isaac moves a car. "*Vrooom, vrroooomm*!"

"Don't drive there!" Eddy shouts. "That's the river!"

Isaac drives on the river anyway.

"Stop!" Eddy screams. "You have to do what I tell you!"

Mr. Greenman, next door, peers through his screened-in porch. How much does he hear us?

David Stein and Isaac get up and run around with their guns. Michael stays on the pavement and does what Eddy tells him. He stops at the traffic lights and moves his car through the city.

Mom drives into the driveway and parks over east Baltimore.

"You're ruining your pants, Eddy!" she yells. "I can't keep buying them. Ruth, you saw him. Why didn't you stop him?"

We have spaghetti and meatballs for dinner, just like every Wednesday. Verna leaves it warming in the oven. Mom makes salad. I help cut tomatoes.

Mom tosses the salad around with dressing. A tomato piece flies to the floor. I bend to pick it up. Mom likes cooking clean. Take out the oil, put it back. Slice the cucumbers, wipe down the counter. Sometimes Mom says I'm a sloppy pig just like Aunt Phyllis and Aunt Irene. Aunt

Phyllis is Dad's sloppy sister. Aunt Irene is Mom's.

Dad comes home later, after he's closed the store, counted the money, and put it in the safe.

Mom eats with her hand on her head, like she has a headache.

"It's good, dear," Dad says.

"The sauce is lousy," Mom says. "What'd we take in?"

She asks the same thing every night.

"Same," Dad says.

I use a knife to cut my noodles.

"Same what?" Mom asks.

"Same as last year," Dad says. "Two hundred fifty."

"Two fifty? Should be higher. Each year it should be higher."

Eddy coughs, then swallows. His whole head bobs.

Mom looks at him. He chews a piece of meatball.

My stomach tightens. Isaac blinks hard, twice.

Eddy swallows the piece, then picks up a spaghetti noodle and sucks it into his mouth. "Mmm, mmm," he hums, as if helping it go down.

"Don't suck the noodles!" Mom yells.

Eddy's mouth goes in a line. His throat moves up and down. He gags.

I get ready to jump, but nothing flies out of Eddy.

He sits at the table after we've all left, finishing his plate. I see him put the rest of his meatball in the table drawer.

The phone rings after dinner.

"Hello, Mother," Mom says.

It's Nana. We clump around the phone.

"Fine. Fine," Mom says. "Uh-huh." Her face gets red. "Here's the kids." She hands the phone to Michael.

"Noodles," Michael says.

"It's spaghetti," Isaac says.

"Yeah," Michael says. He kisses the phone. "Bye."

Isaac grabs it. "I want a holster, Nana."

"No guns!" Mom yells.

"I want a holster," Isaac whispers. "For sticks. *Puh.*" Isaac kisses the air. He gives the phone to Eddy.

"Hi, Nana. Yeayuh. Meatballs."

"Meat*ball*!" Mom shouts.

"Yeayuh. I ate meatball. Can I come?" A bubble comes out of Eddy's mouth. "Bye-bye, Nana."

I take the phone. "Hi, Nana."

"Rutie! How are you, sweet girl?"

"I'm fine, Nana."

"Guess what I have for you?"

"What?"

"A butterfly necklace from Herbert." Nana's brother Uncle Herbert makes jewelry. "Don't tell Mommy, Rutie. Shhh." Nana likes to keep secrets from Mom.

"Is Eddy coming, Nana?"

"If Mommy and Daddy let him," Nana says.

"With me?"

"Eddy can't come alone, Rutie."

"I want to come alone."

"We'll see, sweet girl. Kiss so I can hear it."

I kiss the phone.

"Hang it up," Mom says.

"I got it, Rutie. I felt it."

Eddy brushes his teeth like his wrist lost all its bones.

"When am I going to Nana's, Ruthie?"

"I don't know. Mom and Dad have to say."

He watches his toothpaste spit.

Last summer I went to Nana's. By myself.

Sunday, Mom and Dad give out allowances. Mine's a quarter. Eddy gets a dime. Isaac's is five cents. Michael doesn't get one. He will in kindergarten.

My cash-register bank is heavy. It opens with a key. Birthday money is in there too, from Grandma and Grandpa Tepper, Aunt Phyllis, and Aunt Irene. Nana is the one who gives presents. But she says, "Save your money for something good."

That bank sits down inside my closet. I only open it for *True Romance* and gum.

"Hallo-oh." Verna is back on Monday morning. She has on bright red lipstick. She changes her lipstick color every day.

"Hi, Vern," Mom says. "Can you make up the hamburgers? And put an egg in the milkshake today."

Mom grabs her coat and lunch and runs, waving, out the door. I want to pull her back. She's gone.

I'm full from breakfast, but I lift the cake cover off to cupcakes. I eat two chocolate-frosteds.

I get in just before the bell.

I hurry to my seat. Jeanie sits in the second row, third seat. She smiles and mouths, *hi.*

Miss Peterson's hanky drops out of her sleeve.

Jeanie looks at me. I giggle. Then Jeanie starts.

Frank Mills and Harry Niderman, in the last seats in rows five and six, moo.

The class laughs.

"Plug it," says Miss Peterson.

Plug it! I bend down as if I'm looking for something in my desk, my face hidden, my shoulders shaking. Oh lordy, I don't want to wet my pants like Donna Morse last week, the puddle spreading slowly beneath her desk before she fled to the bathroom. Lucky for her she's short and sits in the front row, close to the door.

Jeanie snorts, laughing hard and trying to hide it.

I fall off my seat to the floor.

Miss Peterson stands over me. "Can you contain yourself, Ruth, or do I have to call your parents?"

"No, Miss Peterson." I scramble up into my seat. "I can contain myself."

Mom and Dad had to come to school in fifth about my self-control. "But Ruth is nice and quiet at home," Mom told Mrs. Crane. Later, Mom gave me the No Jeanie punishment for a week.

I take out a sheet of ruled notebook paper (I can't look at Jeanie) and begin writing sentences with the week's spelling words, which are the states:

Michigan is shaped like a mitten.
The TV stars live in *California.*
Nana's house is in Baltimore, *Maryland.*
Chicago, my home town, is the biggest city in *Illinois.*

Closed shut like a refrigerator, I write neatly on the lined paper.

After dinner, I help Dad do dishes. He washes. I dry. Just the two of us, which makes me start telling my news of the day about spelling the states and starting on wax begonia plants in Science. Dad takes his soapy hand out of the water without turning any other part of him and points it in my direction. His soap-drippy fingers are like a goose's beak when he opens them, shuts them, opens them, shuts them, opens, shuts, opens, shuts, fast, sign language for: clam up your stories, hold your juicy tongue, you're clogging my ears.

I'm quiet after that. I dry the dishes and put them carefully one on top of the other, turning my back to Dad so he won't see a crybaby.

GET LOST IN A BOOK. That's what the poster in the library says, and it shows a big book with boys and girls walking into the pages. I used to wonder, what if those kids got lost and never came out?

Saturday, I run to Jeanie's with the new *True Romance.* She's waiting on her porch.

"Lookit," Jeanie says. She points across the street.

Nuchi Kneehigh is peddling his big three-wheeled bike. He's a man with a little head who makes funny noises. We don't know his real last name. We call him Kneehigh because we think it sounds good with Nuchi. We know his first name because his mother stands on their front porch and calls into the air, "Nuuuu-chi!" when she wants him home. Nuchi's parents are old.

"He's like Eddy," Jeanie once said. "Retarded."

"Eddy can do things," I said. "And he doesn't look strange."

We're afraid of Nuchi and go quickly into Jeanie's house. Inside, we make fun of his groaning, then laugh and cross our legs to stop the pee.

Sometimes Nuchi walks with his father. His father holds his arm and talks to him. I don't hear those soft words.

Mom roars the vacuum cleaner into my room.

"Ruth, you finished reading these?" she yells above the noise. She bumps the vacuum at my bookcase. "We can sell them in the store."

"Those are my books, Mom!"

"Clutter!" Mom says. She roars the vacuum out.

"Let's put socks in our bras when we get to your house," Jeanie says Wednesday after school. We like to pad our chests, then stand sideways and look in the mirror. Cotton anklets work best. Nylon dress socks don't do a thing, and knee socks make us look too bumpy.

"Square dancing tomorrow," I say. "Eugene Brandon."

Jeanie makes her eyes wide.

Maybe Eugene will look at me if my chest sticks out.

"Let's wear our socks to school tomorrow," I say.

Jeanie giggles.

In my room, we stuff in the cotton anklets and write a story about a boy and girl making out on a bed. Then it's time for Jeanie to go.

I walk her to the back porch. "Want to eat over?" I ask.

"With Verna?" Jeanie asks.

"No, with Mom and Dad."

"No thanks," Jeanie says.

Fish for dinner. Eddy looks for bones in every bite.

"See how he eats, Billy?" Mom says. "He takes more out of his mouth than he puts in."

"No bones, Eddy," Dad says. "Mom took them."

Eddy stares at the chewed fish pieces on his plate. I look at the white gobs. The whole table looks at Eddy's fish.

I take my eyes away and try to think of something. Mr. Grimm in Science gave each of us a plant. We each have our own.

"My begonia plant is leaning toward the sun."

Mom looks at me, then darts her eyes to Eddy. His fork with fish is going into his mouth.

Jeanie and I walk into Miss Peterson's room, and the boys snigger. Miss Peterson leads us out into the hall.

"You girls need to go to the bathroom and get whatever you have attached to your chests out of there."

Jeanie and I bump each other, giggling, on our way to the bathroom. In separate stalls, we take out the socks, then ball them in our hands. I stuff mine in my desk as soon as I sit down.

Miss Peterson's writing "Sixth-Grade Class President" on the board.

Donna Morse's hand shoots up.

"I nominate Ruth Tepper."

We use first and last names for nominations.

I can hardly hear Steven Rotman and Larry Simmerly nominated, because I'm floating up near heaven.

It's hard to keep my eye on Eugene and square-dance at the same time, but I mostly do. He's always on a "bow to your partner" or "bow to your corner" and doesn't see. If I had those socks, he'd have his eyes right on me.

"Eddy, leave that chalk and come get the bread."

Mom's just gotten home and is fixing dinner. I can't wait to tell my president news. I set the table. I'll tell when we are sitting.

Eddy comes in and washes his hands. Then he stands still, like he's thinking where the bread basket is. He goes in the pantry. I go in, too, to get napkins. Slowly, Eddy takes a few slices of rye bread out of a plastic bag.

"That's not enough," Mom says, like she has eyes in the back of her head. "Your father eats bread with his soup."

Eddy unwraps the plastic bag again and takes out two more slices. He walks stiff-legged to the table with the bread basket.

"Isaac! Michael!" Mom calls out the back door. "Come in and wash your hands."

The water runs for a second in the downstairs bathroom.

"Show them to me," Mom says.

Isaac and Michael come in the kitchen and stick out their hands.

"The backs are filthy! Do it again. And do it right this time."

"Whooaaa!" Isaac hollers.

"Hush!" Mom says.

Dad comes home and goes upstairs with his little slip of paper. It's the day's take, how much money they made in the store. He enters the numbers in the ledger.

"What'd we take in?" Mom asks as soon as he sits down.

"Do we have to do this now, dear?" Dad asks.

I think the same thing. I have my news.

"What'd we take in?" Mom persists.

"Two hundred forty." Dad sips his soup.

"How'd we do last year?"

"We're down."

"That's bad. That's bad." Mom shakes her head. She stands up and carries her soup plate in the kitchen. She brings out the lamb chops.

I worry about the lamb chops. It's better when we have spaghetti. Or fish. Things don't get as ruined.

"What's bad?" Dad says. "We have a roof over our heads.

We're eating mushroom soup and chops."

I stack the rest of the soup plates and bring them in the kitchen. Then I sit down and fold my hands. I'll tell Mom my news and she'll be happy.

"I was nominated—"

"Billy, look!" Mom shouts.

Eddy is taking chewed pieces of lamb chop out of his mouth and putting them around his plate.

"Looks like a bunch of dead flies," Mom says.

"Don't waste," Dad says.

My stomach squeezes.

"Eat up every bit," Dad says.

Eddy has his fingers at his mouth.

"He's doing it, Billy."

Dad takes Eddy's fingers away from his mouth.

"I can't swallow!" Eddy's face is red.

"Take another piece out of your mouth and you'll sit here all night!" Mom screams.

I try a forkful of mashed potatoes. It stays inside my cheek. Isaac and Michael stop eating.

"Eat!" Mom barks at them. "I'm telling you, Billy, I can't take this!"

Eddy's mouth is in a funny line. He throws up.

"Jesus!" Mom pushes out her chair and runs in the kitchen. She comes back with a rag.

I jump away from the table. Isaac and Michael jump too. Dad keeps eating.

"You have to learn to eat!" Mom yells.

I shut my eyes, but I hear Eddy's squeaks and Mom's

hollow thumping on his back.

Mom yanks my arm. "Sit down!" she screams. "Finish your supper!"

I fall into my chair.

Dad gnaws a lamb bone. Eddy's white. He isn't eating.

Mom points her finger at him. "Leave the table!"

Eddy climbs the two steps to the landing, puts out his hand for the wall, then goes up to his room.

"Nominated?" Mom looks at me.

I try to swallow my potatoes. Some still stick. "I was nominated sixth-grade class president."

Mom snaps her fingers. "Here's luck," she says.

"That's fine," Dad says.

"Yes," I say. Any more questions? That's what Miss Peterson asks after Current Events.

I move my eyes a little to see around the table. The boys are looking at me. They don't have any more questions. What about Mom and Dad?

"We need more departments," Mom says.

She's thinking about the store again and selling books to students.

"We have History," Dad says. "The professors told the students."

"We need Engineering, those big, fat books. Go to the Engineering Department … Sit up, Michael!" Mom growls.

Michael lifts his head. I try to lift up mine.

"I went to Engineering last week," Dad says. "The chairman said they use the university bookstore."

"Oh, brother!" Mom says. She grabs her plate and takes it to the kitchen.

"I'm talking, dear," Dad says.

"I know. I just can't listen."

"When am I going to Nana's, Ruthie?"

Eddy moves his toothbrush up and down, quiet with his weak wrists. He still smells like throw-up.

"Never."

"When?"

"You can't go. Because you're ruining."

"I'm not ruining."

"You are. Everything."

Saturday, Dad drags us to Grandma and Grandpa Tepper's. Mom gets to stay home with a headache.

Dad sits in the back room with Grandpa and talks and talks. Grandpa knocks his pipe tobacco out in the wastebasket by his chair. He calls Dad "son."

I can't stand it in there. I go in the bedroom to look at Grandma's silver hairbrush and comb on a silver tray. She's in the kitchen feeding the boys saltines. Her brassiere is on the bed. It looks like something from a hospital, big and pink with hooks, like you'd put on a broken leg.

When we leave, Dad bends down to Grandma, and she

reaches her arms up around him.

"My Billy," she says, her eyes closed, her eyebrows fuzzed together. She looks like she's in heaven.

Dad forgot to mention I was nominated.

When I'm president, I'll stand up in front of the class and everyone will look at me. I'll wear new suede loafers and a sailor blouse Mom will buy me. At dinner, Mom and Dad will ask, "So, Madame President, how was your day?"

Miss Peterson says to wait at her desk while she dismisses the class.

"Thank you for waiting, Ruth," she says. "I've discussed your nomination with the other teachers"—she means Mr. Bannis in Gym, Miss Roberts in Library, Mr. Carney in Social Studies, Mr. Grimm in Science, Mr. Gulden in Music, Miss Vanderhoffen in Art, and the teacher in Home Ec—"and while we all agree you are nice and smart, we don't know about your behavior, Ruth. You do too much giggling and antics."

Miss Peterson's hanky pokes out of her sleeve.

"President means self-control, Ruth."

I nod my head and look at the board. Miss Peterson erased the math but didn't clean it. What about Mom and Dad? How will they punish?

Maybe Bartlett Elementary could catch on fire and they'd stop having class presidents.

I tell Mom my teachers said I was nice and smart. And about antics.

Mom doesn't care about nice and smart. "That's not good," she says, and goes on slicing tomatoes. Then she says, "No Jeanie. For two weeks."

Dad gets home from work and hears it. "Better mind your p's and q's," he says. He takes off his shirt. He looks bigger in his short-sleeved underwear. I kind of duck my head.

After school, I bring a chair in next to Verna. She has the ironing board up by the radio in the kitchen. Verna irons everything in our house that can be ironed. She listens to her programs and keeps her Chesterfield cigarette burning in an ashtray on the board.

I like to hear Verna talk about Curtis and Curtis Junior. Curtis Junior is in fifth grade and likes the movies.

"Did you go last weekend?" I ask.

"We saw *A Star Is Born*," Verna says. "Curtis Junior liked it."

I could catch the bus and meet them in the lobby sometime. Then we'd go in and share an armrest, my arm next to Verna's, Curtis Junior on her other side. Every once in a while Verna'd lean into me and whisper about the movie.

I get to the part in *Tom Sawyer* when he and Huck crept in the church to their own funeral. The minister said nice things and everyone cried.

I start thinking about my funeral and people admiring me out loud. Mom and Dad would be nearly dead themselves from their broken hearts.

"There was no one like her," I'd hear them say. Their sobs would drown the music.

Steven Rotman wins class president. He's a slow, quiet talker. I would have had too many antics. (I looked it up in the dictionary—antic: an attention-drawing, often wildly funny act or action.) I like the part about wildly funny. It makes me think of Lucy.

We clear the table after cake. Eddy brings in one glass at a time.

"You're so slow," I say. I poke him.

"Stop that!" Eddy yells.

Dad hitches up the electric train Nana sent Eddy. We watch the train go round and round the oval track, passing the miniature house and tree over and over again. Dad's the only one who can run it. He puts a smoke pellet in the locomotive's chimney and we watch it puff little white clouds.

Dad goes in as usual for his Saturday afternoon nap.

Nancy Feller and I have our legs beneath my rug, braiding fringe and listening to the radio, on low so Dad can sleep. He's dog-tired and needs it. Mom's out buying groceries. Isaac and Michael are at David Stein's. Eddy's driving cars through Baltimore.

The doorbell rings. It can't ring again and wake up Dad. I run down to get it, fast.

Two boys hurtle off the lawn and down the street. Is one Eugene?

"What was that?" Nancy whispers. Saturday afternoons we talk in whispers.

"Two boys running," I say. I don't tell about Eugene.

Nancy's ahead of me in the braided-fringe department, so I get to work. Doors creaking and evil laughter are on *The Shadow* radio show. I'm glad my legs are underneath the rug, but I miss Jeanie.

The bell rings again and Dad's door bangs open. He runs through the hall and down the stairs.

Nancy and I stop braiding. I hold in my breath.

I hear the front door open. Someone outside is yelling,

"Ruthee! Rutheeeee!"

"Get out of here!" Dad shouts.

I hurry downstairs and peek over Dad's shoulder. Frank Mills and Harry Niderman are dancing on the lawn.

"Ruthie! Ruthie! Ruthie for president!"

I could pop out Harry's glass blue eye and stop his smiling.

Dad starts down the steps outside. "Don't you ever . . . !" he snarls.

Dad runs.

Those boys stick still on the lawn, their round eyes on a running man. Then they take off.

Dad stretches his hand to Harry.

My arm goes up.

Dad grabs Harry's shoulder. Harry's real blue eye looks wild.

Run! I shout in my mind.

Harry bursts away.

"Don't you come back!" Dad yells.

The boys are far off running. Safe.

I jump back from Dad's hard breathing. He stomps up the steps past Nancy coming down, her mouth wide open.

I listen for Dad's door to shut.

Nancy's outside, practically flying down the walk.

I go upstairs and put my legs beneath the rug.

My back feels open. I pull the rug and slide it with me up against the wall.

At recess, Jeanie and I go out to the playground. I can't look at Frank Mills or Harry Niderman.

"Nancy Feller's telling everyone your dad's crazy," Jeanie says.

Nancy's with two other girls by the fence, poking their fingers through the wires.

I run over to her.

"Quit talking about my dad!" I yell.

Nancy stares at me. She pulls her ear.

I grab her collar.

"Let go!" she hollers. "You're crazy like your dad!"

"Your mom has rat's nest hair!" I scream.

I whip that pipsqueak Nancy around.

Kids come over.

"Hit her, Nancy!" someone shouts.

Our feet stir up the dust.

"Get her, Ruthie!" someone yells behind me.

Nancy's face is wet and dirty. We'll never be friends again.

I finish up *Tom Sawyer* and start *Heidi*. That girl lived with her grandfather on a mountain.

"What'd we take in?" Mom asks.

"Three hundred," Dad says. "We're up."

"How much?" Mom says.

"Fifty."

"Mmm," Mom says. She sips her tomato soup.

"Can we have Mama and Papa Sunday lunch?" Dad asks.

Mom's eyes almost close.

Dad puts down his spoon.

"I work," Mom says.

Dad rubs his finger on his chin.

"Does Mama?" Mom asks.

"You know, dear."

"Does she?"

"They're old," Dad says. "They're tired."

Mom stands up. "Mama's tired," she says.

"Dear?" Dad twists his napkin.

Mom heads for the back hall closet.

Dad starts to stand. My shoulders are high.

"Tired?" Mom grabs her coat. "*I'm* tired, Billy. Sick and tired!" She slams out the back door.

I hear the car start. I run after her in the dark.

"Mom! Mom!"

The car's going down the driveway.

I rush over to it and pound on the hood. "Mom!"

Mom backs out fast. Her headlights curve away into the street.

Mom!

The breakfast room light shines on the driveway. The boys' faces press on the window.

I stay in the driveway and twist around in the cold,

looking over the dark fence at Greenmans', then back at the window light. The boys' faces are gone. My feet move in the cold like I'm going somewhere instead of staring down the driveway.

Lights blast at me. I leap away as Mom drives in. She bangs out of the car, past me, into the house. I stand a while by the ticking car, then follow her inside.

Donna Morse has to stand on a chair so we can see her picture of Christopher Columbus for her Famous Person report. When she's finished, Miss Peterson asks, "What were your references, dear?"

Donna waves a book in the air.

"Is this how we talk about references, class?" Miss Peterson asks. She picks up a book and waves it in the air.

My laugh blurts out. I fall off my seat to the floor.

"Is Ruthie crying?" Donna asks.

Miss Peterson stands over me.

I can't get up because my laughs are gasping out.

"Is she?" Donna asks.

Miss Peterson points to the door. "You need to go out in the hall and settle yourself."

Then I'm standing. I've never been sent to the hall before for busting out laughing without my self-control.

Mr. Grimm in Science says we can bring home our wax begonia plants. I pack mine in a paper bag, which it peeks right out of.

"Dirt near the pot," Mom says, "and it's in the waste-basket."

I put that plant on my windowsill for photosynthesis. Sunlight helps it grow. The waxy leaves reach up two panes, plus some head for the sill.

The phone rings after dinner.

"Hello, Mother," Mom says. I move in next to Mom. "The kids are here."

I hear the sounds of Nana through the phone.

"Meatloaf," Mom says. "No … No … I've tried every-thing. He'll never gain."

Mom's mouth gets tight. She slams down the phone.

"She says she'll fatten him," Mom says, banging out cake bowls and the mixer on the kitchen counter. "She says *she'll* fatten him!"

Last summer, Nana made me steak every night. And she always had cantaloupe, which she called melon. Her refrig-erator was so full, I worried I wouldn't be able to shut the door. Her rooms were crowded too, with sofas and paint-ings. And her bookcases were stuffed. Vases of gladiolas everywhere. Her closets were jammed, and her underwear loaded up her bureau drawers, every color, matching sets, some like rainbows. Some were even pleated, or lacy, even the underpants were pleated. Everything smelled like Nana. Her perfume.

And Nana took me shopping and bought me a green suede suit and a red parka. She said I looked nice in those new clothes. Then she told me things about her life. She'd started dating since Umpah died last year.

"Murray is a nice man," she said. "He's a butcher, but he's a nice man. He takes me dancing."

She showed me his love letters tied in a pink ribbon.

"Umpah never took me anywhere," Nana said. "Not even a restaurant. He had such a bad haircut, I wouldn't go with him anyway. She's like him."

Nana meant Mom when she said "she," but Mom has nice hair.

"So who's your boyfriend?" Nana asked.

"I don't have one."

She laughed. "Soon, soon. You're young yet, my darling."

Nana took me to her store every day. She rang up student books and spiral-bounds while I matched the greeting cards with envelopes. Before I went home, she let me have whatever I wanted from the shelves, all the Johns Hopkins University stuffed animals, pencils, and pens my arms could hold.

Mom stretches out on the couch and reads *Woman's Day* magazine. She only sits back on Friday nights. She turns pages like firecrackers. Dad reads the paper.

I have four of hearts and Isaac four of clubs, so we have war with two cards face down, third one up. Isaac's seven beats my three. Dad makes us call it Peace.

"This one's nice," Mom says. She holds the magazine up to Dad. A woman has on a plaid dress and patent-leather high heels.

"Mmm," Dad says.

"Do my feet, Ruthie," Mom says.

I go to get the Jergens.

Mom reads as I massage. "That's good, Ruthie," she says.

I'm proud to make Mom happy. But I hate the smell of Jergens mixed with her feet. And I don't like touching her corns, those hard yellow buttons on her toes, or the bottoms of her feet like a scratchy stone.

The phone rings. Dad gets it.

"Hello … Oh, Mama." Dad's voice fills up with honey. "I will."

I look up from Mom's feet. Her teeth press on her lips. Her eyes lock on my eyebrows.

Mom carries in something silver before I shut my light. "Lay back," she says.

Mom brings her knee on my stomach, her other knee pressing down my arm, and then she plucks me.

I swing my loose arm at Mom's hair. My legs wham against the bed. "Watch it," Mom says, "or I'll poke you."

Mom plucks and plucks like stinging ants, her hard eyes on my eyebrows.

"Now you'll be prettier," Mom says. She leaves.

I sit up. I go look in the bathroom mirror.

Underneath my new small eyebrows, red skin is stinging.

"Ruthie." Eddy knocks on the door.

"No!" I scream and bang it.

"Hallo-oh." Verna has on dark orange lipstick and a tan hat.

"Hi, Vern," Mom says. She grabs her lunch in a wrinkled brown bag and hurries out the door.

"What's that lipstick, Verna?" I ask.

"Pumpkin Glow," she says. "I'm thinking about Halloween."

I lean into her on the way to get on my coat.

We talk, talk, talk, and talk in the back of the class before the bell rings, me, Jeanie, and Sonya Rice. Our hair is so close, we make each other electric.

"You have new eyebrows," Jeanie says.

My eyes get stinging.

Jeanie gives me a candy corn. I pop it in.

"My Mom …," I say. Then I get breathless.

Dad carves the pumpkin on newspapers spread over the white enamel table in the kitchen. He digs his knife in around the stem, his arms bare in his undershirt, then he lifts off the top and scoops out the seeds. He carves a scary face and pins on green pepper ears. Dad's pumpkins are the best.

Jeanie and I dress as ghosts. Eddy's a ghost too. We have to take him with us trick-or-treating. Isaac and Michael go with David Stein and his mom. Those boys are pirates.

It's dark out. Eddy grips my hand, but I pick his fingers off. He can walk behind us.

It takes him forever to go up and down people's steps. He puts each piece of candy slowly into his bag.

"Hurry!" I yell at him umpteen times.

"I am," he says in his loud, flat voice.

Then he trips on his sheet and his candy scatters over the ground. He picks up each piece, dusts off the dirt and leaves, and puts it slowly back in his bag.

"Jesus!" I say.

No porch lights at Mrs. Hart's. She died Tuesday, then had her funeral. She used to give us two toffees apiece. I won't miss that much.

When we get home, we empty our candy on the kitchen

table. Isaac and Michael's piles are biggest because I had that stiff-legged ghost Eddy.

"What are those leaves?" Mom asks.

"Eddy dropped his candy when he fell," I say.

"I thought you were holding him," Mom says. "Two pieces for you tonight. Everyone else gets three."

I pick out two Sugar Daddys. They'll last centuries.

"Put those back," Mom says. She gives me two Mary Janes, those puny candies.

Mom puts the rest of the candy in a wooden bowl above the refrigerator. We can't reach it unless we pull up a chair.

"Get to bed," Mom says. "We'll be back in an hour. We have to visit Harts'."

Mom and Dad usually stay home on Sunday nights, but they always go see mourners.

When they leave, I turn off the kitchen lights.

"Mom and Dad are visiting the dead on Halloween," I say.

My brothers look scared.

"Spooooooky!" I moan. I turn the lights back on.

Isaac and Michael grin. Eddy looks scared.

I want to scare Eddy more. For some reason. Maybe because he's easy to scare. Or because he's ruining our family.

"Go upstairs, Eddy," I say, "and put on your pj's."

"Are Isaac and Michael?" he asks.

"They'll be up soon."

Eddy slowly climbs the two steps to the landing. I hear

him go up the stairs, his hand brushing the wall.

"Let's scare Eddy," I say to the boys. "We can blindfold him and stick his fingers in stuff and tell him it's dead people."

"Yeah," Isaac says.

Michael stands there.

I open the refrigerator. There's half a tomato in wax paper and a bowl of cherry Jell-O with canned fruit Mom made that afternoon. Milk, eggs, and part of a salami are in there, too. I take out the tomato and Jell-O. Then I go in the pantry and grab a rag off Mom's rag pile.

"Eddy," I call up the stairs. "Come down."

Eddy has on his cowboy pj's, with the hats and lassos. He's holding his teddy.

"Come here, Eddy. I want to show you something."

He follows me into the kitchen.

"I have to blindfold you first."

"What for?"

"You'll see." I make the blindfold tight. "Give me your hand."

His hand is warm and dry. The nails are bitten way down.

I push his hand in the Jell-O. He makes a little cry of surprise.

"This is Mrs. Hart's brains," I moan. "She's dead, but her brain is still alive."

Eddy's arm stiffens.

I take his hand out of the Jell-O, and he tries to pull away.

"Hold him, Isaac!" I say.

Isaac grabs him around the waist. Michael holds his arm.

I jam Eddy's fingers into the tomato.

"This is Mrs. Hart's mouth," I say. I move his fingers around in the pulp. "She's licking you. Now she's going to bite you!" I squeeze his fingers as hard as I can, weak, silly fingers, always picking at his food. The boys hold him.

"I don't like this!" Eddy hollers. "I don't like this!"

I put the tomato down and undo the blindfold. I wipe Eddy's fingers. He's crying.

"It wasn't real, Eddy," I say. "We were only trying to scare you."

Isaac and Michael stare at me. Eddy's crying, holding his teddy.

"Go up to bed," I tell them.

I put the food back in the refrigerator and clean the kitchen until it's spotless. I feel sick. The Jell-O is a mess. Mom will be mad.

I go upstairs to Eddy's room and sit on his bed.

"I'm sorry, Eddy." I lean over and hold him. He has his teddy on his cheek. "But don't tell Mom and Dad. If you tell Mom and Dad, Mrs. Hart will get you."

That makes me sicker.

Next day I watch Eddy eat his cereal and walk to and from school behind me. I watch to see if what I did is on his face. His face is like a blank.

Mom and Dad work late, so he can't tell.

On *I Love Lucy*, Lucy's baby Little Ricky cries so loud, the upstairs neighbor with the long thin face comes down and tells Lucy she has to move.

"Oh, no you don't," says Lucy.

"Oh, no you don't," Eddy says. "Huh, huh, huh. She said, 'Oh, no you—' "

"Hush!" Isaac says.

That night I dream baby Eddy cries in his crib and his fingers get squeezed between the slats and Eddy cries and cries louder.

We start frogs in Science. Mr. Grimm has three terrariums on the shelf under the windows where the wax begonias used to be. We decorate the terrariums with moss and rocks and water bowls. Mr. Grimm puts in the frogs. I don't know how he can touch them.

We give the frogs names and take turns putting in the hamburger.

I decide to touch the one called Lenny. He seems friendly.

I tell Mr. Grimm Lenny's back is smooth without the Jergens.

"Jergens?" asks Mr. Grimm.

I worry Eddy will tell Mom and Dad next night at dinner. I get ready to run outside to Jeanie's. But Eddy just chews his lamb chop like a rabbit, his mouth twisting in short, sharp movements. He swallows hard and doesn't tell.

"Did you go back to Engineering?" Mom asks.

"No," Dad says.

"Don't you want that department?" Mom asks. She looks like she's ready to heave the peas.

Eddy picks up the bone and tears at the fat, his mouth pursed like he's kissing. He makes quick nibbles around it.

"Billy, take that bone away from him," Mom says. "He has to eat real food."

"He's okay, dear," Dad says. "He's eating the fat."

"Take it away! If you don't, I will!" Mom leans across the table and yanks the bone out of Eddy's hand.

"Don't do that!" Eddy cries.

Dad slams his hand on the table.

"Whooaaa!" Isaac hollers.

I leap up and grab the bone out of Mom's hand. I throw it on the floor.

"Leave him!" I cry.

I run upstairs and fall down on my bed.

Mom fills up my doorway. She points her finger at the stairs. "Come down now!"

I slink past her, watching her hands.

Dad points his finger at me. “Don’t you open your mouth like that again.”

His sturdy finger juts, black hairs on his knuckles, hairs on the back of his hand. His hand could crack me, the sound like a rock.

I take the garbage out to the alley, past Eddy driving on the cement. It’s nearly dark. The wastebasket clanks my legs with lamb bones and empty milk bottles inside. My foot crunches something hard.

“Don’t do that!” Eddy screams.

I look down.

I’ve crunched one of Eddy’s cars. A blue convertible.

“You broke it!” Eddy cries.

“I’m sorry, Eddy.” I pick it up. The wheels are sideways. “I’ll fix it.”

“You can’t. It’s broken.”

“I’ll try to fix it.”

I empty the garbage into the alley cans, then bring the empty wastebasket inside. Eddy stands up and watches me.

I take the car to my room and bend back the wheels. A piece of metal is apart. I tape it. I drive the car on the wooden floor beside my rug. It drives a little wobbly.

The car doesn’t go right. I lie down on my rug and push my face in it. I cry about the wobbly car.

After, I get up and wipe my cheeks. Then I go outside to Eddy.

"It's okay now," I say.

Eddy holds out his hand.

"But it's a little wobbly."

Eddy drives the car. "*Errrrrrrrrrrrrr.* It's okay," he says.

He drives the blue car through Baltimore.

After school, we stop at Cunningham Pharmacy. We don't have money, but the clerk gives Eddy chalk for free.

Saturday supper Mom asks Dad about going to the movies.

"Not this week," Dad says.

"What do you mean?" Mom asks. She grips her glass.

Dad digs in his pockets and puts four pennies on the table. "That's it. After bills and food."

"That's it?" Mom asks. "That's it? Do you expect me to sit here night after Saturday night with you and your stubble chin and wisps for hair? Are you kidding me?"

Mom stands up from her chair.

I could run to the back door and block it.

Dad rubs his cheeks. He doesn't shave on Saturday. He puts his hand on his head.

"Do you," Mom hollers, "expect me?" She leaves the room and bangs around in the kitchen.

Dad drops his napkin. He carries out the tomato plate.

"Where do you want the tomatoes, dear?" he asks.

"Leave them!" Mom shouts.

"I'll put them in wax paper."

"Leave the tomatoes!" Mom screams.

I hear a crash. Then a thud.

"Oh, my God," Mom says. "Billy!"

I stick at the table, then I run into the kitchen.

Dad's face is on the floor. His still body in Saturday clothes practically covers the linoleum. The back of his head is bloody.

Mom kneels beside him. Her hands are on his shoulders. "Billeeee," she moans.

I can't move.

A paper bag with metal sticking out is on the floor.

"Whoawhoawhoawhoa!" Isaac hops in and out of the kitchen.

Eddy's fingers move like twigs on a windy tree.

"Billy!"

Michael lies down on the floor.

Dad stirs. "Mmm-fahmmm."

I don't understand him.

Then Dad's still.

Move again! Move again!

"Billy!" Mom shouts.

"What?" Dad says.

"Oh, Billy." Mom lays her head on Dad's back.

Dad rolls over. He looks nice with his open eyes. "What was it?" Dad asks.

Michael sits up.

"Daddy," Eddy says.

"I thought it was eggs, Billy," Mom says. "I thought it was eggs in the bag."

I kick the bag and Dad's wrench peeks out. Mom didn't know Dad's wrench was in the bag when she threw it.

I go outside to Jeanie's, but I walk past her street three blocks to Farnsworth, then left by the Buick dealer. I don't go in Woolworth's. I run across at the light at Bartlett Elementary, past the Chinese restaurant where we ate once. Farnsworth goes on and on. I'm like a walking machine. My feet move fast on the sidewalks and across the streets. I pass concrete buildings. One says Bob's. One says Delsey's.

I've never walked this far. A dog is in the doorway of an apartment building. Mom gave our dog away. Its dirty hairs everywhere.

Mom threw that wrench. Did Dad fall down from his feet and—*smack*—hit the floor? Or did he crumple down on it?

It's quiet out. Not too many trees. My feet are hurting in their loafers, so I turn home. The sky is gray. The sidewalk is.

Up in my dark closet, my cash-register bank scrapes my leg. My skirts flutter all around, my eyes, my cheeks.

Next day, after Jeanie's, I stop in Woolworth's and look at

lipsticks. Those bright colors make me warm.

One time Nana's lipstick on my cheek looked like Miss Peterson's stamp for perfect spelling.

In Handwriting, we write letters to Famous Americans. Miss Peterson has us drop down two lines after the date and two more after the address. We can choose any Famous American we want. I choose Lucy.

16245 Morton
Chicago, Illinois

November 15, 1954

Lucy Arnaz
Hollywood, California

Dear Lucy,

I am in sixth grade at Bartlett Elementary School. I really love your show. My favorite is when you and Ethel are working in the candy factory and stuffing your mouths with chocolate. I laughed so hard I almost you know what. My brother Eddy likes you too.

Could you send me an autographed picture?

When did you decide to be on TV? I've already decided I'm going to be on it.

Your friend,

Ruthie Tepper
(we both have names that end with "ee")

P.S. How is Little Ricky?
P.P.S. Do your mom and dad watch you?

Miss Peterson puts our letters on the board for Parent-Teachers' Night. I copy mine so I can send it in the mail. Most of the boys write to baseball stars. Harry Niderman writes to Dwight David Eisenhower, President of the United States. He starts, *Dear Ike*, and Miss Peterson doesn't make him change it. Mom and Dad say no first names for grownups.

Jeanie writes to Doris Day. "She's so cute," Jeanie says.

Lucy is cute too, with her curly hair and open lipstick mouth. But she's mostly funny.

Mr. Grimm in Science wants us to see a frog's back legs. He takes out the one called Lenny and holds him on his desk. We come around, tall kids in back. Mr. Grimm holds the frog gently and stretches out his rear leg, but Lenny pushes out of Mr. Grimm's hand, onto the desk, then to the floor. He leaps around the room, his little sides quaking.

Harry Niderman chases him. I run after. Then Harry pounces.

"Lookit," Harry says. He stretches Lenny's back leg and practically pulls it off.

"Mr. Grimm!" I holler.

I want to run away from Science and Harry pulling Lenny, a frog, like a weaker boy who can't make anyone stop it.

Mom and Dad leave for Parent-Teachers' Night, and I go upstairs and water my begonia. It reaches up past three panes and drips down lower over the sill, growing bigger in the sun, like it's the boss.

In the morning, Mom barely looks at me. She makes her lunch on the kitchen counter, slapping peanut butter on pumpernickel, then she cuts two slabs of spice cake with buttercream frosting and wraps them in wax paper. I want to ask, did they see my Lucy letter and did Miss Peterson tell nice things about me?

"You like Miss Farnham, Eddy?" Mom says.

Her sudden words make me jump.

Eddy chews his cereal.

"Pay attention," Mom snips. "Do you like your teacher, Miss Farnham?"

"Yeayuh."

"She's a good one," Mom mutters to the sink.

Miss Farnham must be on a visit from heaven with golden hair and small eyebrows for Mom not to criticize.

I'm working on my country report, France, when I hear Mom on the phone. I creep downstairs and sit on a step close to the landing.

"She says he tries, Mother. He tries hard. He just can't do some things."

I know she's talking about Eddy.

"She had his maps up … I don't know … She says the kids make fun …"

Then Mom cries.

I want to beat up the whole third grade.

Mr. Grimm in Science says Thanksgiving is Beaver Moon, the November moon for Indians. He says they had other names for moons, like Hunger Moon is February. Maybe the Indians called it that because it was winter and they were hungry. Like I'm hungry sometimes, even when I'm full.

We see a film in the auditorium called *Pilgrims' Feast*. Mr. Carney in Social Studies shows it to third through eighth. Eddy comes in with the third, standing up straight in the line. He knows how to do it.

Mom throws paprika on the turkey, raw and white, waiting for the oven. I peel potatoes and stare at it, weak in the roaster.

Thanksgiving dinner, Dad gives Mom white meat first, then Grandma and Grandpa Tepper. Good he remembers.

Michael laughs and looks at Isaac. Isaac chews fast, like a rabbit, and picks turkey pieces out of his mouth.

"Isaac!" Mom slams her hand on the table.

Eddy's spit-up comes out.

Grandma Tepper lifts off her seat, then falls back down. "Oh!" she says. After that, she pokes at her food, at her turkey, cranberry sauce, and mashed potatoes.

But no one says, "Can't you stop yelling, even for Thanksgiving?"

The day after Thanksgiving, I drive down to the store early with Dad. Mom comes later. Dad always talks to me in the car about when he was a boy, like stories from the Bible. Mom never tells about hers.

Dad puts me to work in the paperback room, arranging the books in alphabetical order by author. It's quiet and dusty in paperbacks. Most of the customers buy textbooks and spiral-bound notebooks in the other part of the store. Sometimes I get a headache from the dust, but I like it in here. Mom doesn't come in and criticize and I don't have to see the looks on customers' faces when Mom yells at Dad for doing something wrong.

Mom eats lunch early, around eleven, because she gets hungry. I eat later with Dad in the executive dining room (that's what he calls it) in the back of the store by the toilet. I like opening the wax-paper packages of sandwich, salted cucumbers, and cake. Dad reads *Publishers Weekly*, and I read a paperback that looks romantic.

"Don't get the pages dirty," Mom says. "We have to sell it."

By the end of the day I'm tired. I want to go home with Mom and not stay the extra minutes while Dad closes up. I get in the car and lay my head back on the seat. Mom puts the empty lunch bag between us. She uses the same bag every day until it falls apart.

She backs the car out of the alley. Her face has a little smudge on it. Maybe she touched the typewriter ribbon, then put her finger on her cheek. She turns on the radio as we drive toward the expressway.

"That old devil moon ..." Mom's singing with the radio.

Her voice is beautiful. About once every two years she plays the piano and sings tunes from her Rodgers and Hart songbook. She studied piano before she got married. She played with the Baltimore Symphony once.

"... in my heart," she sings.

"You sing like a record star, Mom."

She laughs.

"And you have nice hair."

She touches my hand a second. "Ruthie."

"If you stop yelling, Eddy might get fat."

It just comes out of me. Maybe because she was singing.

Mom's face turns white, her lips stiff. Her eyes go flat. She looks like she's wearing a mask.

Why did I think I could say it?

I watch her hands. I could fall on the floor to get away.

The song on the radio peters out. The announcer gabs about a furniture store. Another song comes on. We drive onto the expressway and inch along in the rush-hour traffic.

Mom raises her hand to brush her cheek. I jam up against the door, but nothing happens.

We drive in the driveway. Eddy's sitting in his winter jacket on the concrete, moving cars over the streets of Baltimore.

"He's ruining his pants," Mom says. She leans back on the seat and closes her eyes.

Then she leans forward and takes the lunch bag out of the car. She walks past Eddy into the house.

I open my door.

"Red light, stop. Green light, go," Eddy says.

"Come in, Eddy," I say.

He doesn't notice. He's in Baltimore.

I get out napkins and utensils, whirling around Mom, trying to stay away from her hands.

Mom wipes the counter. She turns the water on hard and talks so I can barely hear her, except "Eddy." I hear his name through all the water. Mom shuts the faucet. She spins around. Her eyes flick past me on her way to the refrigerator. She stands inside the open door like she forgot why she was there.

"We almost lost him," Mom says.

Monday night, three chairs are empty. Isaac is at Steins' for dinner. Mom and Dad work late.

Eddy talks like milk spilling and no one mopping it. He looks at Michael while he eats. "Michael's eating his soup up, Ruthie."

"Mmm."

"Michael's using his napkin, Ruthie."

"Uh-huh."

"Ruthie, Michael's nice and clean."

"Eddy's teeth are loud," Michael says.

Eddy's teeth sound like a slower woodpecker when he chews.

"Let's just eat," I say. "Then we can watch Lucy."

"Huh, huh, huh, Michael. Lucy."

Eddy laughs like soft dots and bubbles with no one in the three chairs smashing.

"How come you keep turning?" Jeanie asks on the way home from school.

"I'm checking Eddy," I say.

"He's always back there," Jeanie says.

"I know," I say.

Mom said they almost lost him. I turn around again. Eddy's walking from side to side like he's on stilts.

Jeanie needs Belgium pictures for her country report. She chose Belgium because it's right next to my report, France. She wants to look in Dad's around-the-world photo album. He used to travel before he was married and had us.

At home, Jeanie runs into Mom and Dad's room for the album.

"Not in there!" I shout.

I run in after Jeanie. The sun is spread on the floor. Books are on the bedside tables. When do they read?

"Come on, Jeanie," I say. Mom and Dad run in and out of this room, not me.

Downstairs, Jeanie opens the album.

"'A Flemish burgher in Bruges,'" she reads. "What does that mean?"

"Sounds like bruise," I say.

Newspaper pictures in the back of the album show Grandpa Tepper and the Free Loan, Dad on an army horse, and Mom signing up for college. I'm standing next to Mom in my "Ruth" T-shirt. Eddy's in the picture, too, in his stroller, eating paper.

Mom has long hair. She smiles at Eddy.

"Your mom's pretty," Jeanie says.

We go upstairs and write a story about a Belgian woman named Lotte with white teeth and secret eyeglasses. She read when no one knew. We look up spellings for "chamber" and "candelabrum."

Lucy's picture comes in the mail! She has her smile and curly hair and words on her blouse: *For Ruthie. Your friend, Lucille Ball.* She looks right at me.

I tape that picture on my wall.

Eddy is climbing the stairs, one step at a time.

I go out in the hall.

"Come here, Eddy."

He stops. "Are you scaring me, Ruthie?"

I go in my room and sit on my bed. My head tingles.

Eddy peeks in.

"You like that picture, Eddy?" I say.

"Yeayuh."

Eddy comes inside my room. He sits on my bed. We look at Lucy.

Mom pokes her head in. "Do you watch that show?"

We're supposed to be in bed when Lucy comes on.

"Because if you do …," Mom says.

I see the TV flying out the window, over the Stickels', past Bartlett Elementary and the store, splashing down in

Lake Michigan.

"No, Mom. We're sleeping," I tell her. Eddy sits quiet. "But everyone knows Lucy. The kids in school. She's funny."

"Scotch tape ruins," Mom says.

I take the picture off my wall and put it on my bedside table.

My room looks a little cozy with Lucy and the plant.

"Can you see him?" I ask.

Verna has the ironing board up. "Right through the window," she says. She has on her lipstick Barely Pink. "That's where my eyes are. On him and his little cars."

"I'm going to Jeanie's. Bye."

But I stick still.

"I'm watching him," Verna says. "You don't have to ask me."

I wait with Jeanie by the Boynton Avenue door.

Miss Farnham, Eddy's teacher, brings out the third grade.

Eddy holds up a paper with lines and bad writing.

"What's that?" I ask.

"Miss Farnham put it up. Nana's street."

Miss Roberts in Library announces tryouts for *Book Parade.* All she says is it's for readers.

Jeanie and I walk up and down her driveway, holding books with the covers facing out.

"*Book Parade* is a fashion show for books," Jeanie says.

Nuchi pedals down his driveway. He stops and looks at the sky.

"Hi, Nuchi," I say.

Jeanie gasps.

Nuchi raises his hand and makes a noise.

"You're getting brave," says Jeanie.

We grab our books and run inside her house.

Saturday afternoon Mom has Isaac and Michael at Sears for pants. Dad is home asleep. Eddy's driving through Baltimore.

I pull the phone into my room and dial information.

"Fanya Ziller, please," I say. "In Baltimore."

I dial Nana's number.

"Was Eddy lost, Nana?"

"What, Rutie?"

"Mom said."

"Is Eddy lost?"

"He's home. Mom said they almost lost him."

I don't hear her.

"Nana?"

Nana stays quiet.

"Nana?" I don't know what to do about not hearing her.

"Mommy was telling you something, darling. That Eddy was a baby with diarrhea. Do you remember, Rutie?"

I don't know. I don't remember.

"He had diarrhea six months," Nana says.

"Is that why he's so skinny?"

"I don't know, darling girl. He was a baby that was sick."

"Did he almost die?"

"Almost, Rutie."

Mom makes soft things when Miss Farnham, Eddy's teacher, comes for dinner. We have cream of tomato soup, tuna casserole, and pie. Mom had some cherries from the tree in the freezer.

"Behave!" Mom growls when the doorbell rings.

Miss Farnham brings Mom a bouquet and a notebook pad for Eddy.

"Do you want to see outside?" Eddy takes Miss Farnham's hand, his pointer finger in the air.

"Not now, Eddy," Mom says. "It's too dark. And it's cold."

"Eddy has Baltimore out there," Isaac says.

"Good for you, Eddy," says Miss Farnham.

"He sits out in the cold," Mom says.

"Is that right, Eddy?" Miss Farnham says. "Then when it

snows, you can draw maps on the notebook pad."

I want to show Miss Farnham my begonia plant and Lucy, but Mom is bringing in the soup.

After tuna casserole, Mom serves pie. First bite, I think I ate a stone.

"What's this, dear?" Dad asks. He takes a little something out of his mouth.

Mom picks two round stones out of her mouth and puts them on her plate.

Was it me being sloppy with the cherries?

"I forgot to pit this batch," Mom says. "Sorry."

It was Mom. My breath lets out.

"Cherry-pit pie!" Miss Farnham says, laughing.

"Cherry-pit pie," Eddy says. "Huh, huh, huh."

Mom's laugh is like a brook in the woods, low and bubbly.

"Look, Michael." Isaac spits two pits on the table.

"Isaac!" Mom's voice is like a bear's. "Put them on the plate."

Isaac puts his pits on the plate, then spits out two more, *tat, tat.*

"Don't spit," Dad says. He grins.

My laugh bursts out.

Miss Farnham puts her napkin to her mouth, giggling, letting out her pits.

We all eat like Eddy, with our fingers in our mouths, but that pie is good. We laugh about it.

I borrow Jeanie's crinoline plus Sonya Rice's, which along with mine makes three for twirls in square dancing. Eugene might like my wide skirt.

Mr. Bannis in Gym lines us up for square dancing, boys and girls separate. My skirt with crinolines pokes out on the girl in front and the girl behind me. I push to the part of the line where I'll get Eugene. He's ninth and so am I. But Mr. Bannis puts the girls from the front with the boys from the back. That's a trick he does sometimes.

Eugene's square is in a corner of the gym, and mine is right in the middle. When I see Eugene look in my direction, I get rhythmic. I twirl my wide skirt and bounce my head. Eugene is like a solemn prince. His arms are thick like a man's and he grins at his partner Joanie in a little way every now and then, his eyes right on her. Joanie Garber smiles back like he's not Eugene Brandon but her brother or her cousin or something.

Saturday morning Mom makes me chop nuts for banana cake while she whirls around cleaning.

Eddy draws parts of Baltimore on Miss Farnham's notebook pad, then he lays the parts on the kitchen floor. He pushes his cars to stop and go.

Mom rushes in with the mop. She stops still.

"I'm cleaning!" she shouts. She bends down and grabs up every piece of notebook paper, crumpling them to her, making them smaller and smaller. She smashes the paper bundle in the wastebasket. "And making cake!"

Mom grabs the chopper out of my hand and chops like crazy. "Not small enough!" she says.

Eddy puts his coat on.

"It's freezing out, Eddy," I say.

Eddy gets his chalk and goes out in the cold.

Mom throws nuts in the batter and beats it all around.

Eddy has to stay home from school with a cold. After three days, he's not getting better. I hear his wheezing all the way in my room. He sounds like a train. Sometimes like a train whistle.

I dress and go in Eddy's room. His breathing makes my fists get tight.

Mom has the radio on the table next to his bed.

"Do you want Arthur Godfrey?" I ask. Arthur Godfrey comes on in the morning with jokes and orchestras.

"No."

Eddy moves a car over the hump his legs make under the covers. He passes the car up over teddy, holding it with his thumb and finger, his pointer up in the air. I could blow that car away, his holding is so light.

Eddy's breathing sounds like motors.

I hear Mom hurry up the stairs. She rushes into Eddy's room. She has on her low-heeled shoes for the store. She puts her hand on Eddy's forehead.

"I made chicken soup," she says. "Verna'll bring it."

"Okay," Eddy wheezes.

She hands him a Chicago map. "Dad brought it."

Eddy smiles. He sticks out his hand.

Mom hurries out of the room. I run after her.

"Don't go!" I say. I grab her arm.

Mom pulls away. "What?"

"Don't go!" I holler.

"He'll be fine," she says. She hurries down the steps.

"Call the doctor!"

Mom looks at me. "Why are you screaming?"

"Stay home! Call the doctor!"

"Stop screaming," Mom says. "Why are you so worried? He only has a cold."

I run down the steps to Mom.

"Don't leave him!" I scream.

"He'll be all right," Mom says. "I'm late." She runs through the kitchen and out the door.

I listen to her car whoosh down the driveway.

I eat two pieces of cherry cake with marshmallow frosting. Verna lets me after cereal.

The Home Ec teacher is pale yellow. I can hardly hear her voice.

I don't want to push my spoon, like Mom does, through the cornbread batter. I sit down. I am done stirring, ever again.

Dr. Rosegard comes at night and gives Eddy a shot. Eddy cries like barking. Then he gets better.

But my throat starts aching.

I get under my covers and read *Poems of the City.*

Eddy comes up the stairs, slowly.

I could wrap Eddy in my blanket and read to him, warm like a little baby.

"Want me to read to you?" I call through the door.

Eddy peeks in.

I hold my covers up for him.

He ducks back. "No," he says. He shuts the door.

I turn off my light with only *Poems of the City* under the covers to hold.

I scared Eddy. I tell it to my mind.

Book Parade tryouts load up the library with fifth, sixth, seventh, and eighth, including me and Jeanie. Eugene Brandon isn't there, so I can act normal.

"*Book Parade* is a TV quiz show about books," Miss Roberts explains. "It's on educational TV and goes out to all the schools in Chicago."

TV! This is my chance!

Miss Roberts lines us up around the room. I move away from Jeanie. I don't want to get antic and knocked out of

Book Parade. I stand in front of 598.2—birds.

"In what book are a mole and a toad friends?" Miss Roberts asks an eighth grader by the door.

I know that one. *The Wind in the Willows.*

I pop in a cough drop. My throat is hurting.

Miss Roberts goes around the room asking questions. If you miss one, you have to go back to your class.

I get "What was Tom Sawyer's half-brother's name?"

"Sid," I answer. Lucky I just read it.

Miss Roberts nods and goes on to the fifth grader next to me.

When there are only ten kids left, Miss Roberts sits us down. Jeanie grabs my hand. I hold hers tight but look away. I can't giggle and get wiped off TV.

"We need five students for *Book Parade*," Miss Roberts says. "Four for the team and one alternate."

She asks us more questions, then says, "Thank you, boys and girls. You did very well. You may go back to your classes. I will post the *Book Parade* team outside the library door in the morning."

At home, I clamp down my mouth and don't say a thing to Mom and Dad. What if TV is like the nomination and it turns out to be nothing?

Next morning I can see over most of the kids at the library door. I stare at the tacked-up paper.

Me! I'm on the team!

Jeanie too! Two girls and two boys. Sam Goodwin in seventh and Ned Sharp in eighth. Steven Rotman, sixth-grade class president, is the alternate.

"I can't miss this," Mom says when I tell her. She lets me call Nana.

"Nana, I'm going to be on TV!"

"What? Rutie, *Ed Sullivan*?"

"No, Nana. *Book Parade.* It's a quiz show."

"You'll win, Rutie. You're a smart girl."

"Thanks, Nana."

"Bye-bye, darling."

"That's fine," Dad says when I tell him. "Just fine." He pats my head.

I feel like I'm flying in outer space and all the stars are singing, *Welcome!*

The phone rings next night at dinner.

"He did? …," Mom says. "He did? … No … No … Oh, brother."

Mom hangs up the phone. She looks at Eddy.

"Why did you lie to Miss Farnham?"

Eddy opens his lips.

"You told Miss Farnham you were going to be on TV."

Eddy shakes his head.

"Then why did she call to ask what time because she wanted to tell the whole class to watch?"

Eddy moves his mouth like his tongue is stretching far

away. He stares at the wall.

"Liar!" Mom shouts. "You lied to Miss Farnham and now you're lying to me! Ruthie's the only one around here on TV. Not you, Eddy. Quit being a liar."

Eddy coughs and grinds his throat.

"I *want* to be on TV," he says.

"That's different," Dad says.

In my room, I think about filling Eddy's lap with candy. Then we could go outside to Baltimore and I'd let him tell me what to do.

At breakfast, Eddy hums down his cereal, background music to my reading.

"Sickening!" Michael says.

I look up. Eddy's cruising his finger under his upper lip, picking up clumps of cereal.

"Michael," Eddy says, "don't say bad things."

Michael looks at Isaac and giggles. "You're sickening, Eddy," Michael says again.

"Sickening," says Isaac. He blinks three times fast.

"Stop that, Michael," Eddy says.

"You're sickening, Eddy," Isaac says.

I slam my book shut.

"Michael," Eddy says, "you're my friend." He gets up and

puts his face near Michael's, one finger in the air. "You're my friend, Michael," Eddy says.

Michael grabs Eddy's finger and squeezes it. "Biting," Michael says.

My eyes get dizzy.

"Leave him!" I say.

Michael looks at Isaac. They giggle.

"You're sickening, Eddy," Isaac says. "And you're too stupid for TV."

"I'm not stupid!" Eddy screams.

Eddy picks up a cake fork and throws it at Isaac. The fork hits the wall and clatters to the floor.

"What?" Verna calls up from the basement.

Eddy shakes his head. "I'm not."

I wait for Eddy at the Boynton Avenue door. Jeanie waits with me. After a while, no more kids come out.

"Where's Eddy?" I ask.

"I don't know," Jeanie says. "I have to go. My mom gets worried."

I'm worried, too. Where's Eddy? Is he lost?

I run in the building. It's quiet in there with no people, just metal lockers and the wooden doors to the bathrooms.

"Eddy?" I say. I feel like whirling around screaming.

He's not at his locker. I peek in his room. Miss Farnham is on the floor. Is she cleaning?

"Hi, Miss Farnham." I want to scream again.

"Hello, Ruth."

"Where's Eddy?" My voice is high.

"He's here."

I go over to Miss Farnham on the floor. Eddy is underneath her desk.

"Eddy says he wants to go to Nana's, Ruth."

Eddy inches his bottom out. "When are we going to Nana's, Ruthie?"

"Come on, Eddy. You can call her when we get home."

Outside the school, Eddy's legs move fast right up to me. I take his hand for home.

We stretch the upstairs phone into my room.

I dial Nana and give the phone to Eddy.

"She isn't here," he says.

"Just wait."

"Hi, Nana," Eddy says. "I'm coming to see you. Yeayuh … When? … Yeayuh."

Eddy hands me the phone. He opens the door and leaves.

I put my mouth close to the phone.

"I scared Eddy, Nana."

"What?"

"Like Lenny in Science."

"What, darling girl?"

"I scared Eddy at Halloween. I had two Mary Janes

because he fell, and Mom said, 'You were supposed to be holding him.' I only got two candies. That's all." I cry into the phone.

"Rutie," Nana says.

"I scared him."

"Ach," Nana says.

"I made him sad that time, but not after."

"How is Eddy, darling?"

"He was scared."

Nana doesn't talk.

"Eddy looked like horror, Nana. Like I cut into his heart."

"You cut his heart, Rutie?"

"I scared him."

"I know."

"Mom always yells."

"I'm sorry, Rutie."

"Bye, Nana."

"Bye, Rutie. Darling girl."

Nana knows. She knows now I was in that mean square dance everyone does around Eddy.

Will she say I can't come?

I slice a piece of lemon cake with lemon frosting and take it to my room. I eat and read *Heidi.* That girl had to leave her grandfather and go to the city. Cake crumbs fall on the book.

"Ruth!"

Mom's home.

I close *Heidi* on those yellow crumbs, soft and sweet.

Thursday, I pull the phone into my room again.

"Can I still come, Nana?"

"Of course, my darling."

"I scared Eddy."

"You were hurt, darling girl, so you hurt Eddy. That's what we do sometimes. Hurt from hurt."

"Do you love me, Nana?"

"Always, darling girl."

Cold air creeps through the window as I water my begonia. Something pink is poking out. I lift up a waxy leaf and sun flies through four thin petals, sparkly. My plant blooms in winter?

We practice for *Book Parade* after school in the library. Miss Roberts gives us questions and we try to answer them. Kids peer in the glass window of the library door and watch. Every once in a while I get so excited with the answer, I jump off my seat. My cough drop flies out one time and sticks to the carpet.

"Don't jump, Ruthie," Miss Roberts says. "Raise your hand. The team should be mature."

She pronounces it "mah-toor."

Saturday is *Book Parade*!

In the morning, I have to keep my brothers quiet so Mom and Dad can sleep. Isaac and Michael jump on their beds, singing bathroom words.

"Be quiet!" I croak.

They quit jumping and stare at me.

"You sound like a bad giant," Michael says.

Am I losing my voice? Will I have to stay home from TV? In bed like Eddy? Will Steven Rotman, sixth-grade class president, take my place? No! Never!

Mom says Dad has to stay home with the boys. She drives me to the studio. She will watch me.

I hope I look nice for TV. I check my pocket mirror. My eyebrows are back to fuzzed.

Mom drives without talking. She doesn't even turn on the radio. Maybe she's nervous, the same as me.

She'll be happy soon. And Dad. He'll tell Grandma and Grandpa Tepper. If there's a parade, they'll stand on the sidewalk and Dad will point at me. If the newspapers have it, Mom and Dad could hold it two days before they throw it out.

Steven Rotman's parents pull into the parking lot the same time we do. They get out of the car smiling.

"It's a great day," Mr. Rotman says. "Smart kids."

Mom looks at me a second, like she's surprised, like does he mean me?

Maybe she'll find out I am. Maybe even say it.

Inside the studio, a lady takes us to a room with two tables in the front and a lot of lights shining on them. A wooden stand between the two tables has a banner draped from it that says BOOK PARADE.

Jeanie runs up to me. "I like your blouse."

"Thanks," I whisper.

"We don't have to whisper," Jeanie says.

"I do," I whisper.

"How come?"

"I lost my voice."

Jeanie's mouth forms an O.

"Don't tell," I say. "This is my chance."

Jeanie nods.

"Your hair's pretty," I whisper.

"Mom fluffed it," Jeanie says. "It's like Doris Day's."

"Except hers is blond," I say.

Miss Roberts is holding flowers. The team from McDougal School heads for the chairs behind their table. Two boys and two girls, like us. But their alternate is a girl.

"They look smart," Jeanie says.

Two of them are wearing glasses. They must have read their eyes sick. No one on our team has glasses.

"Teams?" says a man with earphones.

We sit down at our table. A man in a blue suit goes behind the stand.

"Mr. Henry will ask the questions," the earphone man says. "And remember, the captain gives the answer."

"Book Paraaaaade!" Mr. Henry begins. "Today we have sixth, seventh, and eighth graders from Bartlett Elementary and seventh and eighth graders from McDougal Elementary. Some of Chicago's finest students."

I look at Mom. She's brushing the front of her blouse.

"Are we ready, boys and girls?" asks Mr. Henry.

"Yes!" everyone shouts. I nod.

"First, McDougal: Who was the star of the Walter Farley books?"

"Black Stallion!" someone from McDougal yells.

"Right!" says Mr. Henry. "Henceforth, team, discuss with each other, then let your captain state the answer. All right, boys and girls?"

"Yes!" shout the McDougals.

They're noisy. Maybe they're nervous.

"Bartlett," says Mr. Henry. "Who couldn't stop the doughnut machine?"

We look at each other.

"Homer Price?" Ned whispers.

We all nod. I nod the fastest.

"Homer Price," says Ned. His voice cracks a little.

"Right!" beams Mr. Henry. "Right from the captain!"

McDougal gets Charles Dickens' *A Christmas Carol*, then we get *Charlotte's Web*.

"Bartlett, what did Charlotte first write in her web?"

"What did she write?" whispers Ned. "Was it 'what a pig'?"

Jeanie and Sam shake their heads.

"I don't know," Ned says.

"'Some pig,'" I croak. Everyone looks at me. Someone on the other team giggles. I look at Mom. Her face is serious.

"R-r-r-right!" says Mr. Henry. "Captains, please."

Mom is looking down. Did she see I was the one with the answer?

Mr. Henry goes back and forth asking questions. The camera rolls back and forth, too. McDougal misses *Robinson Crusoe* and we miss *The Five Chinese Brothers* and *The Hobbit.*

The last question is ours.

"Bartlett," says Mr. Henry. "Why were Mary Poppins, Uncle Albert, and the children on the ceiling?"

"She had her umbrella," Jeanie whispers.

"Laughing gas," I whisper, low.

"I can't say gas," Ned says.

"Because she had a magic carpet," Sam says.

"No, she had a carpet bag," Jeanie whispers.

"I don't know," Ned says.

I lean into them and growl, "Laughing gas."

"I don't know," Ned says again.

I stand up.

Mom puts her fingers on her cheek. She moves them a little over her eyes.

I bend down to Ned on my weak legs. "Laughing gas," I whisper right into his face.

"Laughing gas?" Ned finally says.

"You're right!" says Mr. Henry. "Well done, team."

I sit down. Mom looks bewildered.

The audience claps.

McDougal beats us by one.

Miss Roberts gives each of us a daisy. "You were wonderful, team!" she says. She holds my chin. "Wonderful!"

Mr. Henry and the man with the earphones come over to me.

"You were very good," the earphone man says.

"She was, wasn't she, Bob?" Mr. Henry pats me on the shoulder.

I look for Mom.

"You were great, Ruthie!" Mr. Rotman says. "You knew the answers."

"Congratulations," says one of the other parents.

Mom and I walk out to the car.

Jeanie runs over with her mom.

"Ruthie was great, wasn't she?" says Jeanie. "Even being sick!"

Mom snaps her head to look at me.

"See you, Ruthie!" Jeanie says.

"Are you okay?" Mom asks when they're gone.

"I'm fine, Mom," I whisper.

We get in the car.

"You were good, Ruthie," Mom says.

"Thanks, Mom." I feel like she is kissing me.

We drive a while not talking. It starts to snow.

"That girl on the other team," Mom says, "the alternate, she had nice hair."

I slump in my seat. What other girl? What about her? It doesn't matter about her. *I* was the one. I knew the answers. Not that other girl.

I start to tell about it. "I knew it was laughing gas, because—"

"Rest your voice, Ruthie," Mom says. "You were good. Too bad the other team won."

Mom tells Dad I knew the answers.

Dad says, "Nice job, Ruthie."

I go upstairs and look at Lucy. She looks back at me, her smiling face and eyes.

"How come your hair's that way?" Jeanie asks.

"No bangs," I say. "It's better now. Like that other girl's."

"Want cake?" Verna asks. I've just come home from school.

"In a minute."

I run upstairs and drop my notebook.

Something's different. My windowsill. It's empty! Bare panes, bare sill, bare wall down to the floor. No green arms reaching.

"Where's my plant?" I yell.

I run downstairs.

"Vernaaaah!"

"What?" Verna says.

"Where's my begonia?"

"I don't know about your plant."

"Where is it?" I yell.

Then I remember. Mom.

I run up to my room and check my wastebasket. It's in there. Stuffed. Arms smashed together. I ease my hands down to the pot and lift it. The plant isn't broken. Each fuzzy stem and waxy leaf springs back to the place it wants. I put my begonia back on the sill, its green arms reaching.

When Mom gets home, I run right at her. "What'd you do to my plant? The dirt stayed in! Not on the sill!"

Mom moves to the closet.

"There was a flower! Why did you?"

"Too darn big," Mom says. "Clutter." She takes off her coat.

I want to leap on her.

"Leave my plant!" I scream.

Mom turns. Her eyes look glittery. She walks into the kitchen. I run after her.

"Leave my plant!" I run over to the counter and pound on it. "Leave it!" I pound on it, right up to the cake plate. "Leave it! Leave it!" I grab the cake cover off and slam it down. I plunge my hand straight through the frosting into the cake and swim my fingers around. I squeeze out a chunk and heave it at Mom.

"I hate your cake!" I scream.

Mom stares down at the frosting stuck to her dress.

I heave another chunk. "Your cake's bad!" I yell.

Mom moves toward me. "Don't you ever …," she says.

I jump away and run upstairs.

Mom runs after me. She chases me through the upstairs hall, into Isaac and Michael's room, into the bathroom, my room, then back in the hall, around and around, bedroom, bathroom, bedroom, hall, bedroom, bathroom, bedroom, hall. Mom breathes hard. She stops. I run inside my room and peek out. Mom's bent over her knees.

"That begonia's mine!" I yell. I slam my door and hold it. If she comes in through the bathroom, I can run out down the stairs.

Mom pulls the door, but I'm strong with it.

Her loud breathing quiets. "Stay up here," she says. "Don't come down for dinner."

I lean over my begonia like a tent, my hands cool on the window.

I hear Mom in the kitchen banging bowls.

A frosting piece falls off my finger to the floor. I pick it up and pinch it, then throw it in the trash.

I listen hard when Dad gets home. I can jump behind my door and slam it, then move my desk in front. The other door to the bathroom, I'll have to lean on strong. I can go under my bed to the corner. He'll move it. I can jump in the laundry chute. I'll get stuck.

I hear Mom say, "Ruthie has a headache. She isn't hungry."

"Ruthie?" Isaac knocks on my door.

"Don't go in there!" Mom yells.

Thank you, Isaac. I say it in my head.

I look out my window into the dark. I wish I could see Jeanie's.

Or tie my sheets to the ground. If I could fly.

I sit down hungry for breakfast.

"No Jeanie," Mom says. Her voice is like a starting car.

She throws wax-paper packages in the brown bag.

Verna comes in the door.

"For a month!" Mom shouts. "Vern, no Jeanie!" Mom gets on her coat and grabs her lunch. "Don't let her!"

Mom runs out the door.

I write my name and the date at the top of the spelling test and number down the left side of the margin one to twenty.

"'Hibernation.'" Miss Peterson gives the first word.

I see Jeanie's fingers tapping her desk for the syllables.

I'll stick with her in school.

Sonya Rice doesn't know about whispering on Saturdays. She talks louder than the radio.

"My dad's sleeping," I say.

Sonya's hands fly to her mouth. "Oh," she whispers. "Nancy said."

Jeanie never told.

"Ruth!" Mom calls.

I close up *Heidi*. I've finished my Sunday chores of straightening my closet and lining up my shoes. Heidi saved rolls in her closet when she lived in the city. I go downstairs and stiff-walk into the kitchen.

Mom's in her housedress, thrusting her vacuum like a sword. She stops and points at the kitchen table. I sit down for the canceled checks.

"Sort them," she says. She stays at my shoulder.

My fingers get slower. I feel like I'm forgetting my numbers.

"You put 1097 after 1098," Mom says. "Fix it."

Dad comes in. He's in his house clothes—paint-spattered pants and shoes and his khaki jacket from the army. "I'm having a devil of a time with that door from the den," Dad says. He's hanging storm doors and windows.

"Who hangs storms in December?" Mom asks.

Dad takes a drink of water, then goes back out.

I hear a crash.

"That's it, Marjorie!" Dad hollers.

Mom runs out. I rush after her.

Glass pieces cover the concrete steps by the den. The wooden doorframe has jagged glass.

"Oh, brother!" Mom says. "Fix it!"

At dinner, we have beans slow-cooked in the oven.

"That door's going to cost us," Mom says.

"Mmm," Dad says.

"How can we afford it with the lousy take?" Mom says.

"We can," Dad says.

"Billy, look!" Mom shouts.

Eddy's taking bean pieces out of his mouth and putting them around his plate.

Dad slams his hand on the table. Eddy drops his fork.

Don't hit, I pray.

"All right, Billy," Mom says. She can see Dad's close to hitting.

After dinner, Dad goes upstairs to write in the ledger. I help bring in the dishes. Slowly Eddy puts the two pieces of left-over bread back in the plastic bag. His fingers aren't strong enough to tie the plastic tight. I help him. He puts them in the pantry.

Mom walks in the pantry with the bean crock.

"You put the bread basket on the bottom shelf! That's where the bean crock goes! How many times have I told you where to put the bread basket? You're so stupid!"

"I'm not stupid!" Eddy shouts.

I hold still by the kitchen counter.

"You're stupid! Slow and stupid!" Mom shouts.

"*You're* stupid!" Eddy yells.

I hear a smack. I look in the pantry. Eddy has his hand on his cheek. He takes his hand away and punches Mom in the stomach.

"*You're* stupid!" he screams.

"Billy!" Mom runs through the kitchen. "Come down *now!*"

Eddy rushes past Mom up the two stairs to the landing, right into Dad, who's hurrying down the stairs.

"He hit me!" Mom cries.

"You hit your mother?" Dad shouts. He grabs Eddy's shirt with one bare white arm and hits Eddy's back with the other. His head, Eddy's head, disappears in Dad's stomach, his stick arms and legs waving. Big on little. Big on little. I don't want any broken bones or broken teeth or broken glass or broken door. Just fixed. Someone fix this, please.

"You—hit—your—mother?" Dad is breathing hard.

"Billy, stop!" Mom yells. She grabs his striking arm. "You're hurting him!"

Stop! I scream with no sound. *This is terrible!*

I pull on Dad's fingers, pull at his fingers closed on Eddy's shirt, pull off each finger, thick, pull each finger off Eddy's shirt and Eddy drops away.

"Run, Eddy!" I scream and Dad grips my arm and shakes me, back and forth, back and forth, and I grab his finger and squeeze it but he has me tight and cracks my cheek, loud, the sound like a rock. The ceiling light is bright.

"Oh, Billy," Mom says.

Dad breathes hard in his white T-shirt. He lets me go.

I run upstairs, past Eddy on the edge of his bed holding teddy.

I go into my closet. I don't come out until it's quiet. The hall is dark. The whole house is.

I go back in my closet and lift my cash-register bank off the floor. I open it with the key. Then I put clothes in a bag.

In the morning I put in toothbrushes and teddy, plus pears and Ritz crackers. I leave out *Heidi* because it's from the library. I put the bag in the garage when no one sees.

Miss Peterson and the class, plus Jeanie, are in a quiet mist. The big windows let in the light, the bright outside. I'm going there.

"Wait here, Eddy." I steer him to the tree near Stickels'. "Don't move."

I slink past our house to the corner, then around to the alley. I peek in our back yard. No one's there. Not Verna, Michael, or Isaac. I sneak in the yard to the garage and take out the bag. Then I run back around.

"Come on, Eddy."

I hurry him to the end of the street.

"Are you scaring me, Ruthie?"

My head tingles. "I'm not scaring you. I'm never going to."

I pull his arm a little.

"We're going to Nana's," I say.

"To Nana's?"

"Mmm."

Eddy's feet move faster. "Did Mom and Dad say?"

"Mmm."

Nuchi is stopped at the end of Jeanie's street. I've never seen him this far from home. Is he lost?

Nuchi makes a noise and raises his hand.

"Hi, Nuchi," I say. I want to get away from him.

"Nuuuu-chi!" his mother calls.

Nuchi makes a wide turn with his bike and pedals back slowly.

"Do you know the way to the train, Eddy?"

Eddy turns left at Farnsworth.

"Do you know the way?"

"Union, Fulton, Jefferson, Lake," Eddy honks. His feet are going fast.

The train announcer sounds like an echo.

"*Track four train 449. Train 449 to Omaha track four. From St. Louis, Indianapolis, South Bend, train 319.*"

I stick my hand in the Ritz box, then pass it to Eddy.

The man across from us is reading the paper, his black briefcase by his feet. I check my purse for the tickets. Good thing I had enough in my cash-register bank to buy them.

"I want to see the trains, Ruthie."

I'm tired from all that hurrying in the cold.

"It's too cold, Eddy."

"I want to."

I see a policeman looking around. Is he looking for us?

"All right. Just a little."

I wish I had on leggings. I stopped wearing them in fourth. We both have on hats and gloves. Eddy's hat has ears.

A train clangs into the station, its giant head leading, breathing and steaming. I feel it even in my numb feet.

"It's cold, Eddy."

"Can't we just see?"

"A little."

"Engine, baggage car, coach car, coach car, coach car, dining car, sleeper, caboose." Eddy honks the cars.

"It's cold out, Eddy."

He walks behind me into the station. I see the back of a policeman. Another one is by the door to the street.

I drag Eddy into a store selling magazines. One of the police is coming toward the woman worker. I duck Eddy behind a counter and put my finger on my lips. Eddy's eyes are circles. He holds my hand. My shoes are standing in dust balls. Peanut packages crackle when the woman wedges them on the shelf.

"Seen any kids?" a man asks.

I know it's the policeman.

"Lots," the woman says. "Which ones?"

"A boy and a girl. Runaways."

Mom and Dad must have called them.

"Keep an eye out," the policeman says. "Let us know."

"I will."

The woman worker stands up from the peanuts box. The policeman walks away.

There's a door behind the counter. Does it go out to

the street? I open it and pull Eddy inside. I close it quietly. The room is cold with no light or linoleum. Just dark and concrete.

"How come, Ruthie?" Eddy asks.

"We have to, because …"

"*Milwaukee, Omaha …*"

We can hear the echo announcing through the door. Mom and Dad never called the police before. We called the fire department once. Mom smelled gas, but it turned out to be a skunk. The police called *us* twice when the store had robberies.

If that woman worker comes in, we'll hide behind the door when she opens it.

"Want some Ritz?" I whisper.

"Yeayuh." Eddy's voice is loud.

"Be quiet, Eddy."

Eddy's eating is loud too, but the woman doesn't come. I want to be out in the light and warm instead of the cold room.

"When are we going to Nana's, Ruthie?"

"Soon. We have to wait for the train."

"When?"

"Eight o'clock."

"Nana's nice, Ruthie."

When Nana sees me, she'll wrap me around and say, "My Rutie, darling girl."

"*... New York City, Philadelphia, Baltimore, Washington, D.C., track nine.*"

"We have to go now, Eddy. They announced it."

I stand up a little frozen.

I turn the doorknob slowly and look out. The woman is behind the counter, ringing up *Life* magazine. Three people are in line.

I push through the door, holding the bag and Eddy. No policemen. We walk out of the store over to track nine. We stand behind a woman and a girl in the line. Eddy's tie shoes climb on the train right behind the girl. The conductor smiles.

Lights shine on the aisle. I can see me and Eddy in the train windows, following the girl.

The woman and the girl sit down. I turn Eddy in across the aisle from them, like we're that woman's children.

Eddy sits back in his seat. "We're on the train, Ruthie." His voice sounds like bubbles.

I take teddy out of the bag.

"Here."

Eddy puts teddy on his chin. His other fingers open and close the ashtray.

The woman stands up and lifts a suitcase onto the high shelf. She sits back down and smooths her hair.

"Mommy?"

The woman bends her head to the girl.

"Can you read to me?"

The woman presses on the little lights over their seats. She takes a book out of her carrying bag. I peek. *Keeko,*

Indian Boy.

The girl leans her head on the woman's arm. The woman's voice is so low, I can hardly hear her.

The train starts up, swaying and knocking. The train goes faster and the knocking gets louder.

A conductor comes in. He takes a ticket from someone.

"Tickets?" he asks. He's at the next row. Does he know?

"Come on, Eddy." I grab the bag and practically pull Eddy out of the seat. We go down the aisle to the other end, away from the conductor. I push open the lavatory door and drag Eddy inside. I lock it.

"We have to stay in here." I'm a little out of breath.

"What for?"

"We have to."

Eddy sits on the closed toilet seat. "I don't know."

"It's okay." I lean against the sink.

"This train has bathrooms, Ruthie," Eddy says.

"We can brush, Eddy." I get out the toothbrushes. I forgot the paste. I wet the toothbrushes in the sink and we move them around.

Someone knocks on the door. I hold my hand on Eddy's mouth.

"In a minute." I try it in a deeper voice.

"All right." It's a woman.

A loud rushing like the noisiest vacuum comes in our ears, then it's quiet. I hold the sink hard when the train turns around a corner. When it's straight, I open the door and peek. The aisle is empty. The conductor is gone.

"Come on, Eddy."

The train is darker. Only the little lights are on. The woman across the aisle has her head back and her eyes closed. She must have worked hard all day.

The girl is turning pages.

Eddy talks to himself, looking out the window. "Bolton, Mason, Eutaw."

The girl closes her book and lies down across her mom. The mom opens her eyes. She bends over her carrying bag and takes out a blanket. She spreads it over her daughter and smooths her daughter's hair. She rests her hand on her daughter's head. Then she reaches up her other hand and turns off the light.

"Eager, Madison, Fayette."

"What are those streets, Eddy?"

"Baltimore."

"Are you sleepy?" I ask.

"No."

"I am." I turn off the lights and shut my eyes. I wish I had a blanket. I feel Eddy bump his head down on my lap.

Nana would say, "My darling girl and boy." And we'd cram into her soft side, slip around on her silk blouse with perfume, and Nana would say, "My Rutie, how you've grown. So beautiful, your hair, your eyes."

I stretch out beside Eddy. My cheek, a little swollen, hurts pressed to the seat. I put my arm on Eddy's legs, and the train rocks me, rocks me.

"Miss. Miss." Someone's tapping my shoulder.

I open my eyes and lift my head. The conductor!

"Where are you going, miss?"

Do I have to tell? "To Baltimore. Our Nana lives there." I told.

"Where are your mom and dad?"

The woman across the aisle looks at me. I open my eyes wide at her. She could say we were hers.

"Did they put you on the train?" the conductor asks.

"No. Yes, I mean."

I want to tug his hand like a begging girl and he'd say, "All right, miss, you can stay here."

"You and him will have to get off in Toledo, miss. Your mom and dad are looking for you."

He sits behind us.

The woman closes her eyes. She strokes her daughter's hair.

I sit straight up, bouncing Eddy's head, but he's still sleeping.

Maybe the conductor will fall asleep, too. He could sleep right through Toledo until Baltimore, and we'd get off and run.

No lights except the red NO EXIT down the aisle above the door.

Eddy's stiff legs walk down the steps. "How come?"

My jaws are tight.

Outside the train, two policemen come out of the dark.
"Here they are," the conductor says.
"Where's Nana?" Eddy asks.
A policeman takes my bag. I hold on to Eddy.
"Where are we going, Ruthie?"
My mouth gets open. "Home."

"Why'd you run?" The policeman next to me sits square against the door smelling like smoky cold. I feel like I'm sinking in the back seat beside Eddy in between the two policemen.

The third one in front drives away from the lighted station.

"I want to go to Nana's," Eddy says.

"What's his name?" the policeman next to me asks.

"Eddy," I say.

"Kids should stay home, Eddy. Right?" the policeman asks.

The driver clears his throat and nods.

Eddy leans against me.

I'm so tired, but I keep my eyes awake looking in the dark.

The policeman rings the bell, and Mom flings open the door. Dad stands behind her. I duck back a little.

"My God!" Mom sobs. She practically falls on me and Eddy. It's hard to breathe in her bathrobe, locked into her like in some strange fairy tale, her soap and lotion smell so close, her body in and out with sobbing.

"Well," the other policeman says, "they're here."

"Thank you, officers," Dad says.

Dad takes Mom's arms off us. He won't hit with the police here. He stares at me and Eddy like he'll never stop.

Mom falls over us again, crying, covering us with a new smell, like feet, but softer. I shiver meeting it.

"All right," an officer says.

"All right, dear," Dad says. He moves us more inside the house.

"Thank you, officers."

"Everything all right?" asks one.

"Yes," Dad says. "Thank you."

Inside Mom's robe, I hear the door shut.

Mom lets us go. "Why did you?" she cries.

Mom and Dad look at me. Eddy's shoe scrapes my ankle pushing next to me.

"Let's go on up," Dad says.

I walk behind Eddy. Dad is behind me. He feels like a wind. Eddy puts two feet on each step, his hand on the wall. Mom leads the way, her bathrobe floating out.

"Time for bed," Dad says.

"Good night, Eddy," I say.

Eddy's hard stick arms go around me. His back feels like a board. I put my nose in his hair.

We came home so soon.

Mom and Dad go in Eddy's room. "We'll be in, Ruthie," Dad says.

I get on my pj's in the dark. I can't see Lucy or my begonia, but it doesn't matter. I have them memorized.

"We were so worried, Eddy," Mom says. "I missed you."

I hear her from my room.

"I went on the train," Eddy says, his voice flat.

After a while, Mom and Dad come in. I sit up in my bed.

"We were so worried, Ruthie," Mom says. She turns on the light. "Why did you?"

I watch her hands.

Dad touches my shoulder. I jerk it. "Good night, Ruthie," he says. He walks to the door. "We're glad you're home." He touches his cheek. "I'm sorry."

Dad knows.

"I'll be a minute, Billy," Mom says.

She sits on my bed.

"Why did you, Ruthie?"

I pull my feet away.

Mom slips to the floor. She lays her head on my bed, her hair spilling on the blanket, like she's my little girl, like she wants me to pat her hair and say, "It's all right, my darling."

I clutch my knees.

Mom lifts her head. She holds it there part way, like she's frozen. "Why did you leave?"

I stare at her.

Then Mom stands up. She moves away from the bed to

the door. She shuts off the light. The light from the hall is on her, stiff in the doorway.

I'm jumpy sleeping and kick my covers around. But no one rushes back in and cracks me.

We stay home from school next day. I open my door and Michael runs away from it, over to Isaac. Isaac stands by Eddy's.

"Ruthie's up," Michael says.

"Where'd you go, Ruthie?" Isaac asks.

"Nowhere."

"Mom cried with a noise like throwing up," Michael says.

"Dad cried, too," says Isaac, "when they called about the train."

"So did Isaac," Michael says.

"You did," Isaac says. He puts his ear to Eddy's door. "I hear him breathe." He opens the door.

"Hi, Eddy," Isaac says.

Eddy sits up.

"Hi, Michael," Eddy says.

"Hi," says Michael.

"You went on the train?" Isaac says.

"Yeayuh."

Eddy puts chewed duck pieces around his plate. Mom looks at them like they're the most darling things.

After cake, Dad says, "So ..." He stares at me and Eddy. "We're glad you're home."

He said that once.

Mom puts her napkin on her face.

I hear those words. I see that hidden face. But I'm in a gray cloud and empty.

Eddy picks up cake crumbs with his finger and puts them in his mouth. He moves his mouth even though he isn't chewing. Then he reaches behind his tongue for something stuck way back. He looks at his stomach.

"My stomach's big, Michael. Right?" Eddy asks.

"I don't know," Michael says.

"You're a good boy, Eddy," Mom says.

Did I hear her right?

"We were so worried," Mom says. She looks straight at me.

Mom switches on my light. I'm just about asleep.

"He's not your boy to take," Mom says, quiet in the doorway.

My words come out for Eddy. "Then quit yelling."

Mom shuts my light and closes the door.

I breathe faster under my covers.

"Where were you?" Jeanie asks. "Sick?"

We walk slowly because of Eddy.

When I tell Jeanie, she sits down on the grass of someone's lawn. Then she stands up.

"We could write about that," she says. "This girl in a cave and a horse comes."

We take each other's hands the way we did in kindergarten through second.

"Ruth!"

I close up *Alice in Wonderland* and go downstairs.

Mom makes me peel apples for pie while she makes crust. She has Frank Sinatra singing on the radio.

Mom's hands go fast, rolling out the dough with strong strokes, back and forth, back and forth, the rolling pin knocking on the pastry board. She lifts the dough into the pie plate. "Finished?" she asks.

I hurry with the apple peel and nick my thumb. Blood seeps on the apple.

Mom grabs the peeler and it scrapes me.

"That hurts!" I cry.

Mom peels faster. "You're making a mess," she says. She turns on the faucet and peels rush around the sink.

I push my thumb under the water to wash the blood off it.

Mom pushes back at me, slapping her rag at the peels, hurrying them down the drain.

I walk out to Jeanie's, my fingers picking at my Band-Aid. The sun setting down is bright on the sidewalk, on the neat grass patches along the way to her house. I ring the bell, but no one's home.

I go off her porch and wade back through the bushes to just under her front window. I'm held in close by evergreens and bricks.

A light goes on downstairs at Nuchi's. They might be having dinner, gentle and quiet.

It's cold out.

Mom grabs my arm when I come in.

"It's dark!" she shrieks.

I whip my arm away. "Screaming!" I shout. Then I hurry my voice to low so Dad won't come. "Screaming and yelling," I practically growl. "Why don't you scream at yourself sometime?" I swipe my cheek. "Why don't ..." My voice gets gargly. "You can't ... Why can't you be like a mom?"

Mom stares like stone.

"But no," I whisper, "your face gets red, and that's it. You're tired, you put your head down and don't look up. And when you do, my hair. My hair is bad. What about it? What can I do? You're gone."

I move my legs up to my room and lie down on my bed. I hold myself around.

Mom comes in.

I close my eyes. My neck still has a place with tears.

She sits on my bed.

Then she gets up and leaves.

Over the days, I finish *Alice in Wonderland* with the screaming queen. I start biographies, *Dolly Madison* first. The dark silhouette pictures hide her face away.

Before winter vacation, Miss Roberts gives out invitations to a *Book Parade* party at her house. She invites me, Jeanie, Sam Goodwin, Ned Sharp, Steven Rotman, and all the moms and dads.

I pass Mom the invitation.

"I'll have to pluck your eyebrows for the party," she says.

"I don't want it," I say. I get ready to run.

Mom drops it.

Mom knocks on my door before the party.

I close up *Clara Barton.* My teeth are tight.

Mom hands me a white box. "Here."

Inside is a new sailor blouse.

"Thanks," I say.

"Try it," Mom says.

I go in the bathroom. Then I come out and stand by the mirror.

"It looks nice," Mom says.

I know it, too.

Mom stands next to me in the mirror. My eyebrows are above hers, and my shoulders. I passed Grandma Tepper in fourth, and Nana just last year. Now my eyebrows go past Mom's.

"Hallo-oh."

Verna comes in to stay with the boys for the party. Her lipstick is soft gold.

"What's that color, Verna?" I ask.

"Peachy Blossoms," she says. "I'm thinking about spring."

Miss Roberts' doorway is crowded when we come in. She's saying hi to Steven Rotman and his mom and dad. She looks nice in her blue dress that matches her eyes. I take off my coat and wait to smile at her.

Miss Roberts' house is mainly pink, especially her lamps. Her little white dog named Simone has bottom teeth that you can always see.

"Ruth is a wonderful reader," Miss Roberts says to Mom and Dad.

"I know," Mom says.

"Those Mark Twain books in the living room ...," Dad says.

We're on our way home from Miss Roberts'.

"You took *Tom Sawyer*?" he asks.

He sounds mad.

"You read it?" Dad asks.

My stomach clamps. "I loved that book," I say.

"Then try those others," Dad says.

Friday supper Dad looks up from his soup. "Papa asked me to come on over, dear, and bring them fish and saltines."

"Mmm," Mom says.

"He said Mama's legs are bad, and would I get—"

"Sit up, Michael!" Mom shouts.

Michael jerks his head up from the table.

"... so I said I'd come by around four fif—"

Mom lifts the tomato plate and bangs it on the table.

"Do you want more tomatoes, dear?" Dad asks.

"No!" Mom screams. "Does Mama?"

Mom's hand is hard and stiff on the plate, like she has to hold it. Hold something. My hand moves toward her plate. I pry her fingers off. My thumb is on the outside of her rough knuckle. I move my thumb over Mom's hand, her bumpy veins. A little piece of skin pricks my thumb going back and forth. Her knuckles like chicken bones, and rough. She needs the Jergens.

Mom breathes quieter.

The table settles like dreaming.

Mom brings her other hand on mine.

I keep my hand very still inside Mom's, like a sleeping mouse afraid to wake up.

Mom presses her hand tighter. My fingers are warm.

Spoons plank down. They've finished soup.

I leave that little nest, Mom's hand, and finish sipping mine.

After cake, we clear the table. Mom puts leftovers in Pyrex and Dad washes the dishes. Eddy brings in one fork at a time.

"Thank you, Eddy," Dad says.

I go upstairs and water my begonia, growing up against the cold, green arms reaching. When it gets warmer, I'll open up my window and that plant will climb out even taller.